HOT BRAZILIAN DOCS!

The night is theirs…

Brothers Marcos and Lucas escaped the *favelas* of Sao Paolo at a young age and have risen up in the world to become two top-of-their-class surgeons. Marcos and Lucas may think they can handle any curveball life throws at them, but when they come face to face with two feisty, fiery women suddenly these Brazilian docs are further out of their depth than they've ever been before!

Hold on tight and experience sizzling Brazilian nights with the hottest doctors in Latin America!

The *Hot Brazilian Docs!* duet by Tina Beckett is available now.

Marcos's story:
TO PLAY WITH FIRE

Lucas's story:
THE DANGERS OF DATING DR CARVALHO

Dear Reader

I'm sure all of you have read stories about long-lost relatives somehow finding each other after years apart. Whether that reunion takes place as a result of social media, an ad in the newspaper, or through the efforts of family and friends, that first meeting is often an emotional, heart-wrenching time. Depending on how many years—or decades—have elapsed, those people might even feel like strangers when they finally come together.

This kind of story provided the basis for Marcos's and Lucas's books, only their tale has an added twist. The brothers grew up on two separate continents, one having been adopted while the other grew up in an orphanage in his home country. Now adults, with different last names, one thing binds them together: a promise they made many years earlier—one they each fulfilled in his own special way. I freely admit to shedding a tear or two as these characters struggled through some heartbreaking memories and reforged their connections to each other and their past.

Thank you for joining these strong men as they learn about love and loss, and as they work their way towards a happy ending with a couple of very special women. I hope you enjoy their journey as much as I enjoyed writing about it!

Much love!

Tina Beckett

The second story in Tina Beckett's
Hot Brazilian Docs! **duet**

THE DANGERS OF DATING DR CARVALHO

is also available this month from
Mills & Boon® Medical Romance™

TO PLAY WITH FIRE

BY
TINA BECKETT

MILLS & BOON

Published in Great Britain 2014
by Mills & Boon, an imprint of Harlequin (UK) Limited,
Large Print edition 2014
Eton House, 18-24 Paradise Road,
Richmond, Surrey, TW9 1SR

© 2014 Tina Beckett

ISBN: 978-0-263-23898-3

Printed and bound in Great Britain
by CPI Antony Rowe, Chippenham, Wiltshire

Born to a family that was always on the move, **Tina Beckett** learned to pack a suitcase almost before she knew how to tie her shoes. Fortunately she met a man who also loved to travel, and she snapped him right up. Married for over twenty years, Tina has three wonderful children and has lived in gorgeous places such as Portugal and Brazil.

Living where English reading material is difficult to find has its drawbacks, however. Tina had to come up with creative ways to satisfy her love for romance novels, so she picked up her pen and tried writing one. After her tenth book she realised she was hooked. She was officially a writer.

A three-time Golden Heart finalist, and fluent in Portuguese, Tina now divides her time between the United States and Brazil. She loves to use exotic locales as the backdrop for many of her stories. When she's not writing you can find her either on horseback or soldering stained glass panels for her home.

Tina loves to hear from readers. You can contact her through her website or 'friend' her on Facebook.

Recent titles by Tina Beckett:

HER HARD TO RESIST HUSBAND
THE LONE WOLF'S CRAVING**
NYC ANGELS: FLIRTING WITH DANGER*
ONE NIGHT THAT CHANGED EVERYTHING
THE MAN WHO WOULDN'T MARRY
DOCTOR'S MILE-HIGH FLING
DOCTOR'S GUIDE TO DATING IN THE JUNGLE

*NYC Angels
**Men of Honour duet with Anne Fraser

These books are also available in eBook format from www.millsandboon.co.uk

DEDICATION

To those who keep their promises.

PROLOGUE

MARCOS HADN'T WANTED his father to go. But he'd gone anyway…just like he did every day.

Sitting in the dust outside their house, Marcos carefully sorted through the load his dad had brought home yesterday. Plastics here. Metals here… *Careful, don't get cut.* A rusty cabinet he and his brother had to drag over to the pile. Marcos had already snuck the screwdriver out of his father's backpack, so he could try to take the cabinet apart.

He had to do as much as possible before Papai came home, because it made something in Marcos's chest hurt to see his dad's hands shake as he tried to fit the tool into the screws—and the scared look he'd gotten on his face when he hadn't been able to.

"Watch your brother." His father's words had rung in his ears that morning, just as they had every morning since he'd seen his mom in that funny box. His dad had looked real scared that day, too. Marcos had just felt sad and hungry.

So he kept watching Lucas, while moving things from one stack to another. His brother was dragging a stick through the dirt, his feet almost black. Marcos frowned. Where were his flip-flops? There were lots of sharp things out here. But Lucas never listened. No matter how many times Marcos told him. He stomped over to his brother and kicked off his own shoes and pointed at them.

Lucas's lips got skinny, but he stuck his feet into the shoes. He was mad. Marcos didn't care. It was his job to make sure Lucas didn't get hurt.

And now he had to make sure his dad didn't get hurt, either.

"We have to hurry." He glanced at the sun, which wasn't as bright any more. "Papai will be home soon."

"I don't care."

"Yes, you do. I heard you today. You said the same thing I did."

"Did not!" Lucas picked up a plastic drink bottle and threw it as hard as he could across the yard.

Marcos didn't argue with him. But before his dad had left this morning Marcos had told him he was going to be a doctor when he grew up, so he could make him all better.

Lucas's head had bobbed up and down. "Me, too. I'm going to be the best doctor in the whole world."

Papai had blinked his eyes several times and then turned away like he didn't believe them. But he would see. Marcos would make himself smart. Then his dad would stop shaking, and that scared look would go away.

The sound of hands clapping three times outside made them both freeze. Papai never clapped to get in. Only visitors did that.

Marcos snuck over to the tall fence and peeked between the cracks in the boards. It wasn't Papai. It was a man in a grey uniform. *"Polícia,"* he whispered.

He started to shake. Just like his dad.

Then the policeman squatted down and peered through the fence, staring right at him…

CHAPTER ONE

HE COULD HAVE heard a pin drop.

Dr. Marcos Pinheiro began the slow, rhythmic countdown in his head as he waited for the patient on the other side of his desk to react.

Her hands slowly tightened on the armrests of the white leather chair.

One...two...three...four...fi—

"N-no more tumor? Are you sure?"

He nodded. "Your latest CT scan came back all clear. No signs of regrowth on your pituitary, *graças a Deus*. And your hormone levels are back within the normal range."

He kept his voice low and soothing, knowing she'd braced herself for bad news and was now struggling to process the fact that her worst fears were not going to be realized.

"Graças a Deus," she repeated, making a quick sign of the cross over her chest.

Fifty-nine years old, with two children and three grandchildren, Graciela Abrigo might have been any number of patients he'd seen over the last several weeks. But she wasn't. And his little invocation of thanking God wasn't one he often made—especially not when talking to his patients.

But Graciela was special. She'd worked in the orphanage where Marcos had grown up—had put up with a lot of crap and acting out from him when his brother had been ripped from his side and adopted by some nameless family. He could still see the flash of fear in Lucas's young eyes.

"Watch your brother."

Bile rose, and he swallowed hard to rid himself of the taste.

He still didn't know what had happened to Lucas. No one by that name had shown up on any of Brazil's registries that he could find—then again, he probably had a new last name now.

But Graciela had assured him that the couple who had come for his brother had been nice. Kind. She'd seen it in their eyes. Lucas would have had a good home. *"Graças a Deus,"* she'd murmured, in a voice much like the one she'd just used.

As kind as this mysterious couple had supposedly been, they hadn't wanted Marcos. Hadn't seemed to care that they'd separated brothers who had still been reeling from their father's death six months after the fact.

He shook himself free of the anger that still had the power to wind around his gut and jettison him twenty-nine years into the past.

It was over. Those years were long gone.

Forcing a smile, he stood and rounded the desk. Graciela had been there for him when no one else had. And he was glad he'd been able to play a small part in doing something for her in return.

Because Marcos Pinheiro always repaid his debts.

And he always kept his promises.

Graciela stood as well and embraced him, cupping his cheeks and kissing his right one in customary São Paulo fashion.

The click of the door opening behind him sounded just as she said, "I have to get back to the home. Thank you, Markinho. For everything."

His smile this time was genuine, even as he tried not to wince at her use of his childhood nickname. "I haven't heard that in ages."

"Then it is time. You will always be little Markinho to me."

Turning to walk her to the door, the smile died on his lips when he saw who'd come into his office.

Ah, hell.

His mind blanked out all thoughts of Lucas and

the past. Hopefully she hadn't heard Graciela's parting shot.

Because Markinho was not the image he wanted to project to those working under him. Especially not to a certain fiery-haired American who'd been "under" him in more ways than one. Actually, she'd been on top, if he wanted to get really technical about it.

Which he didn't. All he wanted to do was forget it had ever happened.

He saw his patient out and then slowly shut the door, turning to lean against it.

Dr. Maggie Pfeiffer. All long legs, luscious curves...and cool, collected efficiency.

"Posso te ajudar?" Marcos spoke English fluently, having made it a point to drill it ruthlessly into his head as he'd attended med school, knowing it was a necessity in today's medical fields. But he chose to address Maggie in Portuguese—though she still struggled at times with the language, even after six months at the hospital.

"Oh...um." After a moment's hesitation, she worked through her answer. "Yes. I have a question about one of our patients's treatment."

Our.

He'd been slowly letting out the reins and giving Maggie more responsibility, especially with international patients. Which served as a blessing, since it gave him some breathing space—time when he wasn't constantly aware of her scent...of the soft, sexy accent when she spoke his language.

The memory of her straddling his hips in the cramped confines of his car as they'd hammered out all the reasons she should be careful about using certain hand gestures caused a visceral re-action low in his gut. One that came on so fast he had to grit his teeth to fight his way through it. Beads of sweat broke out on his upper lip as the images of that day swept over him.

Get past it, Marcos.

Forcing his thoughts back to the here and now, he focused on a safer subject: her language abili-ties.

She was doing well, but there were still treat-ment methods she wasn't familiar with...words she struggled to translate in her head. And hearing her refer to his patient in a joint sense made some-thing in his stomach shift. His eyes followed suit, moving lower for a split second to where Maggie's fingers were unconsciously fiddling with one of the buttons on her silky green blouse. Just below the swell of her breasts. Breasts that had filled his hands to perfection.

Hell.

He dragged his gaze back to her face. "Which patient are you referring to?"

"Ana Leandro."

"What's the question?" He pushed away from the door and took a step closer, his eyes narrowing when Maggie moved back a pace, her bottom hitting the edge of his desk. She glanced down at the wooden surface in surprise then reached back and gripped it with both hands, sending all kinds of images ricocheting through his skull.

Very bad images. Of him. And her...

And that desk.

"You have her physical therapy scheduled for once a week. But she's handling it well. Should we bump it up a bit and be a little more aggressive?"

He struggled to remember the patient's diagnosis, closing his eyes to pull up a physical description of the young woman. Marcos had always been a visual learner, committing things to memory in a way that most people couldn't. There'd been no books at their house, so he and his brother had both become adept at memorizing images and then trying to outdo the other.

He wondered if Lucas could still...

It didn't matter. Nothing did, except keeping his mind trained on the task at hand.

"Where's her chart?" She'd come into the room

empty-handed, which was unusual. The woman was nothing if not meticulously efficient. Even the way she'd made love had been a study in efficiency—not a movement wasted. Not a sound made. Only the reflexive closing of her eyes as she'd lowered herself onto him one final time, the tightening of her hands on his shoulders and the sudden soft convulsions of her body telling him that she'd climaxed.

And her *frieza,* that cool, aloof manner that seemed so at odds with someone who had hair the color of burning embers had made the experience even hotter. Made him want to break through that icy wall and make her lose all control.

His body reacted again, and he took a steadying breath as he waited for her answer.

"Ana is in PT right now. I thought we might go and see her together."

"Together…" His brow lifted. "Right now?" Why he felt the need to goad her was a mystery. Maybe it was irritation at the reaction she seemed to draw from him every time she was near.

Maggie's lips parted, her teeth sinking deep into the lower one.

Okay, so maybe his thoughts weren't the only ones edging toward a very dangerous cliff. Although that might not be a good thing because he might just be tempted to leap over the edge, and take her with him.

"I would like us to go and see her. Together." Said as if she needed to clarify what she wanted to do with him.

Pity.

"Graciela was my last patient until after lunch, so…" He put a hand on the doorknob and pulled, the normal chaotic sounds of the hospital slipping through the opening and grounding him.

Just like they always did.

Silence was not his friend. Marcos was used to sound. Lots of it. His earliest memories were of his home in the *favela*, where the thin walls and corrugated metal roof had done nothing to dampen the sounds of life…and death. And afterwards, the orphanage where he'd been raised had been a boiling caldron of activity, the noise levels sometimes rising to the point where his ears had rung.

Which made Maggie's quiet manner and even quieter lovemaking seem otherworldly…as if a cool marble statue carved by some gifted sculptor had come to life. What would she think of his world? His background?

Not something he wanted to dwell on.

"After you." He motioned toward the open door.

"Oh. So you'll see her?"

"That is what you were asking me to do." He allowed the corners of his mouth to lift as his gaze trailed across her pale skin. "Isn't it?"

She colored, right on cue. His lips edged higher. At least that was one reaction he could wring from her. There were things that even Maggie Pfeiffer couldn't hide. The pucker of her nipples as he'd unbuttoned her blouse and let his fingers trail over her skin. The moist heat he'd discovered at the apex of those lean thighs as he'd pushed deep inside her.

"Yes. Of course it was." She let go of the desk and slid her palms down the fabric of her grey pencil skirt, drawing his attention once again to areas he should avoid. At all costs.

She swished by him, the economy of her steps matching everything else he knew of her. Maggie didn't waste her time on things that weren't important.

Like her own wants and needs?

Maybe that's why she'd fascinated him from the time he'd laid eyes on her all those months ago.

Brazilians were a hot people. And he'd grown up in an atmosphere where that heat had been fanned by the winds of desperation. People in the *favelas* clawed out happiness wherever they found it and devoured it whole. You didn't wait to be asked. You took. Eased whatever pain you had…whether it was in your belly or in your loins.

And right now that pain was definitely south of his stomach.

But he'd sworn to himself that Maggie was off-limits from now on. He'd had her once.

And that had been more than enough.

Maggie's legs were a quivering mass of nerves, but she forced them to keep moving down the long hospital corridor…to keep her body in motion. If she didn't stop, he wouldn't see her shake.

What the hell was it about the man that intimidated her? What was it about those brown eyes that made her insides heat?

Just because he reminded her of the dark knight from her dreams who came to rescue her from those horrible nights that seemed to never end—the ones where she tried so hard to keep quiet—was no excuse. Which was probably why she'd fallen prey to Marcos in the first place.

No. Prey was the wrong term. It had been nothing like that. Nothing like those nights from her past.

How she'd ended up kissing Marcos as they'd discussed a cultural mistake she'd made was still foggy in her head. Maybe it was some strange, unknown effect of embarrassment. One minute they'd been in his car in the staff parking garage, getting ready to drive to the apartment the hospital had secured for her. Nervous, she'd dropped her water bottle, and it had rolled into the well by his feet.

As they'd both leaned down to retrieve it, their cheeks had brushed, and heat had bloomed inside her. Marcos's head had come up as if he'd sensed her reaction, his brown eyes staring deep into hers. The rest had been a blur of movement. A hot, fast shifting of clothes. His hands on her hips, lifting her up and over him, undoing the buttons of her blouse—she swallowed hard—sliding into her. Her body's instant response.

The whole thing had probably been over in less than five minutes.

The repercussions, though, were still with her a month later.

The only thing she knew with certainty about that day was that it had been a mistake.

A lapse that could never happen again. He was a doctor. Her boss, for all practical purposes, even though she carried the same title he did.

Why had she been so bewitched by him? She should be used to Brazilians by now. Her hospital in New Jersey had had a high concentration of them, so many that she'd often grown frustrated by the language barrier and had struggled to understand cultural norms so different from her own. When a chance had opened up to come to Brazil to intern under a world-renowned neurosurgeon, she'd fought to be included in the program. And had won the coveted spot.

All she needed was to ruin it by letting the man's deadly good looks get beneath her skin.

Like she'd already done a month ago?

She quickened her pace, trying to outrun the memories.

That had been a moment of weakness. She'd been insecure in the language and had used a hand gesture with a patient that had sexual connotations. Marcos had shot her a look, eyes narrowed in speculation before swooping in and correcting her faux pas. And later that day, in the darkened interior of his car, he'd shown her exactly what that misused signal meant.

And he'd been loud. So loud.

Heavens!

She swallowed, her stomach quaking at the memory.

But just because she'd made one mistake, that didn't mean she should follow it up with another.

She was a smart woman, not a shrinking, naive teenager—at least, not any more. She'd already seen what Dr. Markinho wanted from her.

And it certainly wasn't her expertise in the exam room.

Which was why she needed to keep that cold shoulder aimed squarely at the man following behind her. Except, judging from the way her butt was growing warmer by the second, she had a feeling the good doctor was looking anywhere but at her shoulder.

"Here we are."

Thank God. She turned to face him at the glass door of the physical therapy room. Damn. Maybe she'd been wrong. He looked perfectly in control, just like he always did—not a dark hair out of place, although a few streaks of grey had gathered at his temples, like clouds before a storm. And the man's gaze was definitely glued to her face, not the slightest twitch of eyes wandering to other places.

Maybe she'd been imagining things.

Or worse…wishing.

CHAPTER TWO

"MARCOS! EARTH TO MARCOS!"

Cool fingers covered his eyes, and someone gave him a quick peck on top of the head, which almost caused him to lose his grip on his first real cup of coffee of the day. For a split second he thought it was Maggie who'd kissed him.

It wasn't.

He gave a soft curse, then twisted his head sideways to dislodge the person's hands. "Sophia, this is not the place."

"*Nossa Senhora.* You're so grouchy nowadays."

His childhood friend dropped into one of the hospital cafeteria's tan upholstered chairs and crinkled her nose in irritation.

Almost as slender as she'd been during their days at the orphanage, Sophia Limeira had looked Marcos straight in the eye when he'd arrived at the state-run home, plopped her thumb out of her mouth and offered the wet digit up to him. He'd just stood there staring at her, trying not to cry in front of his little brother, who kept asking where Papai was…when they were going home. Marcos had already grasped the truth of their situation from the moment he'd seen the policeman on the other side of the fence: they weren't going home. Not ever.

Sophia, as if recognizing a lost soul when she saw one—had stuck to his side like glue from that moment on. Had even followed him into the medical field. Marcos, in turn, had protected her when she'd been little—still felt the need to protect her now that she was an adult. And even though she griped about it constantly, he had a feeling she secretly liked the fact that someone cared.

He took a tentative sip of his coffee as he tried to formulate a response to her declaration. "I'm not grouchy. I'm busy."

With a flourish of her fingers, four rectangular slips of paper appeared, splayed apart like a hand of cards. "Too busy to go with me to the ballet? I won four tickets from a promotion they were having at Printemps."

"Printemps? What the hell is that?"

"Wow, Marcos. Such language." She sighed and stuffed the tickets back in her bag. "It's a department store down on 25 de Março. I know you've seen it."

A bargain-hunter's paradise, the huge shopping district in the center of São Paulo was a chaotic beehive of activity on the best of days…and the last place Marcos ever ventured, if he could help it. The area could also be dangerous. "You went down there by yourself?"

Sophia rolled her eyes. "I'm not a kid any more, remember? We've talked about this."

"We did. And you agreed to take someone with you when you shopped."

"I did. I took the American girl you have working for you. She'd never been." Her brows came together in rebuke. "After six months, can you believe it? You should have at least offered to show it to her."

Yeah, right. He could just see that happening. Maybe he'd ask her tomorrow, in fact. Marcos pinched the bridge of his nose, feeling a headache coming on.

Maggie was the last person he wanted Sophia hanging around with. His friend might take it on herself to do something crazy.

"Anyway," she continued, "Maggie said she'd go to the ballet with me, but that leaves two tickets. She said she was sure you'd want to go as well."

Something crazy. Like that.

His hand dropped back to the table, eyes narrowing. Somehow he doubted it had been Maggie's suggestion that he go. "Sorry. Can't make it."

"You don't even know what the dates are yet."

It didn't matter. No way was he going to the ballet with Sophia and her new BFF.

He tried to pry the truth out of her. "Did Dr. Pfeiffer actually mention me by name?"

"She did." Sophia drew an X across her chest with her index finger. "*Juro.*"

I swear. Fitting, since he'd like to do a little swearing himself.

"What did she say, exactly?"

"Well, I said I might ask you to go along with us, and Maggie said, 'Do that.'"

He gave a short laugh, relief washing through him. "It's called sarcasm, Soph. Americans use it a lot."

Okay, well, that cleared up that little mystery.

Undaunted by his lack of enthusiasm, she leaned forward. "Did you know Americans also use this…" she made a circle of her thumb and forefinger, shielding the sign with her other hand to keep it hidden from fellow diners "…to mean that something is good? Maggie said she accidentally used it with a patient a while ago."

"Yes. I know." Marcos pushed her hand down

with a frown and held onto it. "That doesn't mean *you* should go around flashing it."

He remembered exactly when Maggie had used that sign. Seventy-nine-year-old Guilherme Lima had come in to ask about his test results, and before Marcos had realized what her intentions were, out had come the finger circle accompanied by an emphatic shake or two of her hand. He'd thought the poor man—whose test results really had been A-okay—had been going to die of a stroke right there in his office. Marcos had thought he might just follow his patient over the edge. But for an entirely different reason. Maggie's innocent demeanor, accompanied by that obscene gesture, had set off a firestorm in his belly that had lasted the rest of the day.

When he'd offered to drive her home with the idea of setting her straight in private so she wouldn't be embarrassed, things hadn't gone exactly as planned. He'd explained why she shouldn't use that sign, and her eyes had gone wide as she'd licked her lips. Another deadly combination he hadn't been able to resist—and hadn't bothered trying. Then she'd dropped that water bottle and leaned forward…

Something he was better off not thinking about right now.

As if he'd summoned her, a flash of red to the side caught his attention, and he swiveled his head to look. Maggie was in line with a tray, but her eyes were on him, following the line of his arm to where his hand still held Sophia's. A frown marred her brow, and something about it made Marcos let go of Sophia in a rush.

A second later, he thought better of it. Had his friend even explained their relationship to her? That he'd been Sophia's sidekick at the orphanage?

Why did it matter? In fact, it might not be a bad thing if Maggie thought there was a little something going on between them.

Which would make him look like a first-class jerk, after those passion-filled moments they'd shared.

As if realizing she was still staring, Maggie yanked her glance back to the tray in her hand and continued through the line, perusing the items behind the glass window at the counter as if they fascinated her.

Unfortunately, Sophia had also spotted her and waved her over.

Meu Deus. Why had he ever thought coffee was a good idea?

With a sense of impending doom, he watched as Maggie made her selection, hunched her shoulders and headed their way, looking very much like she was facing a slow and painful death.

Well, join the club, *querida*. You're not the only one.

Maggie had wanted a simple fruit cup, hoping to make up for the fact that she'd skipped breakfast that morning. What she *hadn't* wanted, however, was to witness her boss holding hands with her new friend, Sophia, who was everything Maggie wasn't: curvy, with flawless tanned skin and silky black hair that shimmered with every movement. The girl also seemed to have cornered the market on flirty smiles, except she did it with a total lack of guile about how that sultry flash of teeth affected the opposite sex. And judging from Marcos's reaction, he'd definitely been affected.

It might even explain why Sophia had been so quick to mention inviting him to the ballet.

Did she have any idea what he and Maggie had done in the parking garage? No, of course she didn't. She had the feeling Marcos wasn't the kind of man to kiss and tell.

But he might be the kind of person who played the field. And there *was* something between these two. She could tell by the way they leaned into each other as they talked, by their easy smiles and casual manner.

Past lovers?

Present?

That thought made having to sit with them that much worse. Because, if the two of them were involved, the last thing her boss would want was for Sophia to discover what they'd been up to a month ago. From the uneasy look on his face, he was thinking much the same thing.

Before she could veer away to another table, however, Sophia leaped up and took her tray, setting it next to hers and then kissing her cheek. Maggie still hadn't gotten used to that aspect of their culture: the kissing—whether it was the casual Brazilian kissing that went on between friends and relatives or, worse, the crazy intense style she'd experienced with the Brazilian seated across from her. Yep, that style of kissing was still kind of foreign to her, since the encounters she'd had in her past life had almost never involved mouth-to-mouth contact.

She sucked down a quick breath as an unwanted memory pushed its way in. She shook it off, her fingertips curving and pressing deeply into the sides of her thighs.

He's dead. The past is dead. Get over it.

Slumping into her seat and wishing she could be anywhere else, she forced a smile. "I didn't realize you'd be here." She gave the offhand remark in such a way that neither party would know who she referred to.

"I come here every morning." The faint amusement that tinged his words made her bristle. She wasn't stalking him, for heaven's sake.

"Really? I only come when my boss asks me to show up at a ridiculously early hour," she retorted.

He glanced at his watch, one side of his mouth quirking. "Six o'clock is hardly early."

"Hmm." The vague noise was meant to be noncommittal, but it caused Marcos to lean back, arms crossing over his chest.

Sophia, seemingly unaware of the tension in the air, spoke up. "I was just telling Marcos about the ballet. And that you were going, too."

Oh, no! She'd hoped any drama involving those tickets would happen out of her earshot.

"When is it again?" Marcos asked, his eyes trained on her face, which was growing hotter by the second.

Sophia glanced at her. "Two weeks from Wednesday."

Lifting his phone off the tabletop, he used a finger to scroll across the screens, probably looking at his calendar. "We have a medical conference starting this Monday."

Something she was trying her best to forget. They were supposed to sit together, since part of the conference dealt with advances in neurosurgery. Marcos said he'd probably need to translate portions of it for her.

The last thing she wanted him doing was whispering in her ear. She'd had that experience once already and didn't need any reminders of what a heady thing it was.

"That's perfect," Sophia said. "Those things never go past five in the afternoon, and the ballet doesn't start until eight."

Maggie wasn't sure what she was supposed to say to that. She'd already promised Sophia that she'd go. But that had been before she'd found out she'd be a third wheel. She wanted to back out more than anything, but didn't want to offend her friend in the process.

"Will it be at the Municipal Theater?" Marcos asked.

"Of course."

Now was her chance to try to wriggle out of it. "Maybe I should just let you guys go and enjoy it on your own."

"What are you talking about? Of course you

must go." Sophia laid her hand on Marcos's arm. "He wants you to come as well, don't you, Marcos?"

"Definitely. I want you to come."

The smooth words were said without the slightest twitch of an eyebrow, but she felt her face flaming back to life. He'd used that phrasing on purpose…knew it would bring up memories of her—with him—as he'd told her he wanted her to do exactly that.

And she had.

She wished she could think of something equally witty and sophisticated to lob back at him, but she couldn't come up with anything that wouldn't be obvious to everyone. Which made her feel like a royal dork.

Besides, how could she refuse to go after her friend had been so excited about winning the tickets in the first place? Nope. She couldn't bring herself to say the words. So she gritted out a smile instead. "Well, I guess that's settled, then."

Sophia gave an audible sigh, then leaned back with a grin. "Exactly."

CHAPTER THREE

"Do THEY HAVE to shave all my hair off?"

Teresa Allen's big blue eyes looked up at her with a pleading expression. The seven-year-old had come in to have her ventriculoperitoneal shunt checked. She'd been having headaches for the last couple of days, and Marcos wanted her in his office right away to make sure the device was draining off the excess cerebrospinal fluid the way it should.

It wasn't. And now Maggie's task was to keep their young American patient and her mother calm while Marcos prepared for the emergency surgery. Once Teresa was anesthetized, however, she'd be able to scrub up and join the surgical team.

Maggie smiled. "No, they won't shave all your hair, only this little spot right here." She drew a U-shaped figure with her fingertip behind the little girl's right ear. "You can comb the rest of your hair so that it covers it once you're out of surgery. But it'll all grow back before you know it."

Her mom, seated beside her daughter, smiled. "Thank you for speaking to us in English. I really need to learn Portuguese, but there are so many ex-pats here I haven't needed to. Your English is excellent, by the way. Congratulations."

Maggie grinned back. "That's because I'm an American, too. And believe me, once I open my mouth, no one would mistake me for a Brazilian, even when I'm speaking Portuguese."

It felt so good to speak her own language. It was also the reason Marcos had left her here with the mother and daughter. And although she knew she deserved to be in that operating room every bit as much as he did, she didn't resent being here. She could remember the times her own mother had held her hand when she'd gone to the doctor to have her inoculations…or when she'd been sick. It was important to feel safe.

And Maggie could remember, down to the minute, when she'd no longer felt that way. It had taken her a long, long time to recover. Even now she wondered if she was functioning one hundred percent normally.

Her ex-boyfriend certainly hadn't given her much reassurance on that front.

But Marcos hadn't seemed to sense anything weird during their brief interlude. Then again, she hadn't been paying attention to much outside of how he was making her feel.

One of the nurses came into the room with a pair of hair clippers. "Are we ready?"

"I think so." Maggie stroked Teresa's head. "What do you think? Are you ready for those headaches to go away?"

Teresa nodded. "I'm really scared, though."

Meeting her mother's eyes, she could see it was taking every ounce of willpower for the woman not to burst into tears in front of her daughter.

Maggie smiled. "I'm going to be with you the whole time. I promise."

"Even during the operation?"

She nodded. "Even then."

Her mom's chin wobbled even more as she mouthed, "Thank you."

Forty-five minutes later, Maggie stood beside Marcos as he carefully examined the shunt valve he'd removed from Teresa's head. "The problem's in here. We'll need to replace it with a new one." Setting the device aside, his fingers followed the path of the tubing down the child's neck and chest, feeling it through her skin. "Everything else seems okay, and she's got plenty of room left for growth. So let's get in and get out."

Maggie busied herself with retrieving the replacement valve and carrying it over to the table.

Marcos took a step back. "Why don't you connect it?"

Surprised, she glanced at him for a second, before moving closer. Taking hold of the lower section of the catheter tubing, she carefully worked it into the connecting port, and then did the same with the upper end. She checked the seals. Hooking it up took less than ten minutes, but it felt good to be doing actual surgery, instead of feeling like a useless hanger-on.

She also realized that she hadn't needed to translate Marcos's words in her head when he'd spoken but had automatically processed and understood them. She gave him a huge smile, only realizing a second later that her mask kept him from seeing it. But evidently he'd seen something in her eyes because he said, "Good job."

It had taken almost seven months, but maybe she was finally getting the hang of this crazy language.

And maybe even gaining the trust of her fellow neurosurgeon?

They finished up the surgery, each of them moving forward and then back to allow the other person to have a turn securing everything in place and then finally closing the incision. Marcos examined the site with a critical eye. "I think that about does it. Let's bring her out of anesthesia while I clean her up."

Marcos gently swabbed the blood from the side of the child's head as the anesthesiologist began lightening the sedation and removed the tape from her eyelids. Within minutes, Teresa's eyelids fluttered.

Leaning over her, Maggie smiled and said, "Can you hear me, pumpkin?"

Teresa nodded her head, her gaze still unfocused.

"That's wonderful." It suddenly didn't matter that she was standing in the middle of a team of Brazilian doctors and nurses speaking English. All that mattered was that this child understood her. "See, I promised you I'd be right here with you every step of the way, and here I am. I've never left your side."

She glanced up to see Marcos staring at her with an enigmatic look. "Pumpkin?"

"It's an endearment." She couldn't help raising her brows in challenge. "Kind of like Markinho."

The whole room went silent for a second or two, and she realized she'd made some kind of serious gaffe.

In a low voice he gritted, "I'd rather you didn't call me that."

Oh! She hadn't meant to insult him, had just been trying to explain why she'd addressed their patient using the name of a vegetable. "Sorry. It won't happen again."

"Thank you." With that, he stripped off his gloves and headed out the door without a word to anyone.

What was with him?

She could no more imagine Marcos being embarrassed by her playful comment than she could imagine herself being. Then again, she didn't know the man at all.

And probably never would.

No one called him that.

No one except his father and his brother. And Graciela, who'd begun using it after hearing Lucas do so. Once his brother had left with his adoptive family, her use of the diminutive form of his name had made him feel cared for—and a little less lonely.

But hearing Maggie say it had made his gut do a slow burn. He knew she wasn't trying to be unprofessional, and hadn't actually been calling him Markinho. But that soft accented voice murmuring his childhood name had made those same sensations go through him that he'd had as a child. Only Maggie wasn't interested in making him feel cared for.

And he certainly wasn't lonely. Not with all the noise and activity of the hospital going on around him.

He'd overreacted. Had stormed out of that operating room like a child.

Like Markinho might have done, once upon a time?

No, he wasn't a child. He was temperamental. He'd heard the nurses use that term to excuse his lack of social interaction.

Because as much as Marcos liked to be surrounded by noise, it was more as an observer than a participant. Except with Maggie, evidently. He found he had to fill the silence that was her with talking…or, worse, groaning.

Like in his car?

The tinted windows had been dark enough to block out everything that happened inside, cocooning them in a private world where anything could happen. And it had. His eyes had been locked on Maggie's face while her eyelids had fluttered closed the second he'd moved her panties aside and found her wet and ready. Her tight heat had massaged his flesh again and again, his words of encouragement every bit as suggestive as the hand sign she'd used with his patient.

And when she'd come…

Hell, she'd exploded within minutes, the sensation taking his body by storm and forcing an audible reaction from him that had left him shaken.

They'd been lucky none of the security guards had been around.

Maggie, on the other hand, had been totally silent. Because of the fear of discovery?

The urge to find out—to have her under him in more private circumstances—swept through his system like wildfire.

He rolled his eyes as he forced himself back to the present and stepped into the staff washroom. He scrubbed his hands and splashed his face, staring at himself in the mirror—and trying not to see Markinho reflected back at him.

Why had she gotten under his skin? Even during the surgery he'd been aware of her every move. Her every word. And when she'd used his name his senses had churned to life.

He had a feeling it wasn't her use of his nickname that bothered him so much. It was what she'd said to the little girl in the operating room.

Marcos had a personal rule that pretty much

governed everything he did. He never made promises he couldn't keep. Rarely made them at all,
in fact. Not after what had happened with his father. Hearing Maggie toss that word around with
such ease—and to a child—without thinking of
the repercussions had struck him as irresponsible.

He was being ridiculous. It was only surgery…
a period of an hour and a half.

And if his patient had regained consciousness
and found Maggie hadn't kept her word?

He switched off the water and turned away from
the mirror. Time to go talk to his patient's family,
although he had no doubt Maggie had already accompanied the girl to the recovery room and made
sure she was settled in. If he knew her—which
he didn't, not at all—she'd also spoken with the
mother and assured her everything was going to
be okay.

Another promise that was impossible to keep.

What was wrong with him today? He didn't
normally brood on the past.

Maybe something about his new colleague
brought it out in him—or perhaps it was those
flashes of something that appeared behind her
blue eyes periodically.

Sadness?

He'd thought it was fear the first time he'd kissed

her. The look had taken him aback, made him wonder if he was acting like a brute.

Probably.

It was why he didn't get involved with staff or any of the nurses. He didn't want tales of his exploits making the rounds.

In fact, he would have stopped with a kiss that day in the car if Maggie hadn't accepted his challenge to kiss him back and awoken something raw and primitive inside him. After that, neither of them had seemed able to halt what had happened.

Marcos huffed out a breath and left the restroom, irritated once again. He had to stop thinking about her. It was becoming almost an obsession. And he didn't obsess about anything…or anyone.

Arriving at the waiting room and finding it empty, he stopped at the nurses' desk. "My patient. Where is she?"

"Wh-which patient?"

The stuttered words drew him up short, making him think about Maggie's reaction to him. Did he engender fear in everyone he came across?

Forcing a softer tone to his voice, he clarified, "Teresa Allen."

The nurse tapped the keys of her computer and said, "Recovery room three."

He strode away before stopping again with

a frown. Turning back to the desk, he said, "Thank you."

"You're welcome."

There. At least she hadn't stuttered that time.

Arriving at the recovery room, he found Maggie was indeed there, along with Teresa's mother. He ignored her for the moment, going over to shake hands with the mom and saying in English, "I'm Dr. Pinheiro."

"You're the one who did the surgery?"

He glanced at where Maggie stood, chin elevated as if bracing herself for whatever he might say. He cursed his careless words in the operating room. "Actually, Dr. Pfeiffer and I both had a part in it. She's already explained what we did?"

"Yes. The new shunt should be okay for a while?"

"For a long while, we hope." He smiled at his patient, who'd drifted back to sleep. "Teresa has to lie flat for the next twenty-four hours, so she'll need to stay here for another day or two."

"Can I stay with her?"

"I don't see why not. It might make her feel more secure to have you here. I can have a cot brought in."

"Thank you." They shook hands once again, and Maggie came over this time.

"You'll let her know I was here?" she asked the mother.

"Yes. She'll be happy to know that. Can you visit her tomorrow?"

Maggie reached out and hugged her. "Absolutely. I'll see you later."

With that she was out the door without a backwards glance at him.

Dammit.

He went after her, catching up to her within a few strides.

"Hey. *Espere.*"

Maggie stopped in her tracks, the sudden halt not making the slightest sound on the polished linoleum floor. She stayed put but didn't look at him. He rounded her still form until he stood in front of her, ignoring everything around him as he stared down at her. When she finally glanced up, the cool indifference in the clear blue depths of her eyes was unmistakable, even to him.

An act? Or was she really not bothered by what he'd said to her? Either way, he owed her an apology.

"I'm sorry." He touched the line of her jaw with his index finger, forcing it not to linger for more than a second on the softness he found there. "I overreacted a little while ago. Markinho is a child-hood name. No one uses it."

"One of your patients did." Her soft voice spoke volumes.

He'd forgotten she'd overheard Graciela call him that a few days ago.

"She's different." He tried to think of a way to explain it that didn't involve talking about his past. "I've known that particular patient for a very long time."

She studied him for a second or two, as if trying to decide whether or not she was going to accept his explanation. "I'm sorry if I embarrassed you. I was trying to explain why I called Teresa 'pumpkin.'"

"No harm done."

Really, Marcos? Are you certain of that?

He wasn't sure of anything, when it came to her.

He forced himself to continue. "The medical conference starts Monday. I'd like us to drive over there together, if possible."

What the hell? Did he really want her back in his car after what had happened? He'd talked about them sitting together during the seminars, nothing more.

She might need help finding the place.

Nothing like having an argument inside your own damn head.

"I think catching a taxi from the hospital might be a safer bet…for everyone."

He couldn't hold back a smile. "Point taken. Tell you what. Why don't we meet here in the lobby at seven and we'll take the subway instead. It stops close to the convention center and we can walk over there together." He glanced at her shoes. Swallowed hard. "Wear something comfortable."

And on that note—trying not to dwell on the fact that her shiny black pumps looked exactly like the pair she'd been wearing that day in his car, or the fact that one of them had fallen off some time during their maneuvering, forcing him to retrieve it from the floor afterwards—he stalked away to get his fifth cup of coffee.

And to hopefully locate his damned sanity.

CHAPTER FOUR

MARCOS MURMURED SOMETHING to the woman seated behind the registration desk at the conference center, but Maggie couldn't hear what it was.

He hadn't said anything else about what had happened during the surgery two days ago—when she'd mistakenly used his nickname in front of a roomful of medical staff. In fact, Maggie hadn't seen much of him since then. But he had left a note at the nurses' station confirming he'd meet her in the hospital lobby this morning.

Riding on the São Paulo subway had been a new experience for her as she rarely traveled downtown, but it had been a fairly simple trip. They'd even found seats next to each other—which Marcos had indicated wasn't always an easy feat. Not that it mattered. He'd been glued to the screen of his phone the whole time, evidently checking and responding to emails.

Despite the quick ride over, they were still a few minutes late for the opening of the convention. Marcos didn't seem overly concerned. These things never started on time, he'd said.

He'd been right. The line behind them grew longer by the second, and she didn't hear anything coming from behind the closed doors to their right.

Maggie was used to punctuality, so the laid-back atmosphere she'd found in Brazil was another thing that was hard to get used to, but it all seemed to work out in some weird way. And the hospital was top notch, up on the latest treatment methods and as spotless as they came. Teresa Allen's impeccable surgery was the norm, rather than the exception. As for the doctors... She glanced at Marcos from beneath her lashes, a shiver going over her. Well, that was something she shouldn't think about right now.

What she *did* know was how fortunate she was to have gotten this internship.

The receptionist handed Marcos two lanyards, along with a couple of printed name tags, and he paused at the table to slide the paper tags into the holders. They'd put an "a" at the end of her name, instead of an "e". Marcos sent her a grim smile as she slipped the cord around her neck. "It seems they think you're magic."

"I'm sorry?"

He lifted the plastic holder from her chest and nodded at it. "*Maggia*...or *magía*, in Portuguese. Magic."

Another shiver went over her as he let the tag fall back into place and donned his own lanyard. She licked her lips, not sure if she dared joke about it. "Well, at least they didn't make the same mistake I did by using your nickname. What does it mean, anyway?"

"Markinho? It means little Marcos." He steered her toward the doorway, which was being pushed open by a couple of dark-suited ushers. "Although I might take exception to being called 'little'. Do you want to weigh in on that?"

Heat flashed up her neck. Oh! He was in quite a mood today. Maybe because Sophia wasn't here to witness his antics. She switched to English. "Don't you think you should be a little more discreet?"

He stopped in front of the doors and turned to face her, ignoring the clipboard-wielding attendant who was tilting his head to try to catch sight of their names.

"Discreet? In what way?"

"Does Sophia know about...what happened?"

Realizing there were people waiting to get in, he held his badge up to the man, who flipped through the sheets and checked something off.

Then Marcos moved through the door, leaving her to catch up.

"Do you mean between us?" He narrowed his eyes as he glanced sideways at her, making his way up the tiers of blue-upholstered chairs in the main room of the conference center. "No, and there's no need to tell her."

Outrage flashed up her back and made her blink. What kind of man was he? "You often do that sort of thing?"

He gave her a strange look. "It depends on what you mean by 'that sort of thing' and your definition of 'often'. But what does any of this have to do with Sophia?"

No one could be that dense. Unless he truly didn't care about the other woman's feelings. "If you two are, um…*seeing* each other, surely she wouldn't appreciate—"

"Seeing?" His brows drew together, and he switched back to Portuguese. "As in *transar*?"

More heat poured into her face, joining the simmering flood that was already at work there. That was one verb she knew. But did he have to be so blunt? She glanced around to make sure no one had heard. "If you want to put it so crudely, yes."

"Sophia and I aren't…" His furrows eased, and he actually laughed, taking her elbow and lead-ing her to a seat in the middle of the auditorium. "She's like a sister to me. We've known each other since we were…young children."

Despite the puzzling pause at the end of his words, a wave of pure relief washed over her, rinsing away the heat that had collected in her cheeks. Okay, so he and Sophia weren't lovers. Although why she should care one way or the other, she had no idea. Except that she didn't want to hurt the other woman.

Maggie knew first hand what it felt like to be racked with guilt over the consequences of someone else's actions. Only her aunt had never found out the truth about her husband—and never would now.

Thank God. It would have killed her to know what he was really like.

Fingers slid across the small of her back, sending a zing of electricity through her. "How about here?"

For a split second she thought he was asking her where she liked to be touched, then realized he was nodding to the chairs in front of them.

Sitting next to him for the next several hours was going to be pure torture if she didn't get her head on straight. She was going to try very, very hard not to ask him to translate anything during the conference. Which meant she'd have to concentrate. A good thing, in this case.

"It's fine. It doesn't matter where we sit."

People were now moving through the auditorium in clusters, talking shop as they went by. Why couldn't she and Marcos be like that? Simply focus on their jobs and leave their personal baggage at home.

Maybe because most coworkers didn't engage in car sex…a fact that sent a worrying tingle through her fingers every time she thought about it. It was the guilt that was causing it. She'd done something she shouldn't have. She glanced down at her hands, checking the length of her nails, just in case.

It was normal for things to be awkward. How could they not be?

She dropped into her seat, staring doggedly at her program. Their unexpected kiss that day had been an almost violent encounter. So much so that the suddenness of it—his hand curling around her nape and then the harsh, desperate press of his mouth against hers—had stormed her senses. The momentary sense of shock at her reaction had rendered her immobile, unable to do anything except let the wash of need sweep over her.

He'd pulled away at that second and stared into her eyes. "*Meu Deus*. You're frightened."

She'd shaken her head, realizing she wasn't. "No."

"Then kiss me back, *querida*…"

A hand touched hers, yanking her back to the present with a start. "I'm sorry, what did you say?"

"I asked which of the seminars you wished to attend. The only one I'd like to sit in on is called 'Sublabial versus Endonasal Surgical Options for Patients with Pituitary Adenomas.'"

She stared at her program, trying to make sense of the words. Not easy with Marcos looking over her shoulder, his warm, mellow scent carried to her on subtle air currents. "I'm here for the language more than anything so whatever you choose is fine."

"Are you interested in any of the other specialties?" He fanned through his book to find the directory. "They've got endocrinology, plastic surgery, oncology, pediatrics…" Reaching over to flip her program to the right page, his fingers brushed hers, causing her to freeze for a second.

She inched her hand away from his, hoping it wasn't as obvious as it felt. "I'm good."

A masculine throat cleared above her, and they both glanced up. Marcos smiled and rose to his feet in response to the newcomer. She tried to shrink into her seat as the two men talked above her, but she was painfully aware that Marcos's brown leather belt with its elegant silver buckle was right at her eye level. Her fingers tingled again, and she forced her gaze to move higher.

Marcos set a hand on her shoulder. "Maggie, this is Dr. Silvano Mendoso, head of pediatrics at our hospital. Silvano, meet Dr. Maggie Pfeiffer. She's here from the States to do a year's internship in my department."

They must get tired of using a title for every single person they came across.

She craned her neck up to smile at the other doctor. Almost as tall as Marcos and with dark curly hair, he gazed down at her. She squirmed in her seat. Standing was out of the question at this point, as she'd be pancaked between the two men if she tried. She settled for lifting her hand to shake Dr. Mendoso's. "Pleased to meet you."

"I haven't seen you around the hospital," he said, gripping her fingers for a fraction longer than necessary.

Up went Marcos's brows. "That's because I keep her quite busy, learning new things."

It had to be the language that made everything sound exotic…and slightly suggestive.

The lights dimmed and then came back up. Dr. Mendoso gave her an apologetic smile and then slapped Marcos on the back. "I'd better get back to my seat before someone decides to steal it. Nice to meet you…Maggie, wasn't it?"

"Yes. Thank you. You as well."

She tried to settle in to listen to the opening speech, not daring to ask Marcos to translate missed words here and there. She caught the gist of the instructions: the explanation of the layout of the building; where to find the refreshment tables between sessions; and who to ask if you got lost.

Lost? She was all that and then some.

Surprisingly, she understood a good deal more than she'd expected to. Several hours later, though, she revised that thought. Her mind felt like Swiss cheese, the gaps in comprehension growing with each change of subject matter. The temptation to lay her head on Marcos's shoulder and drift off was strong.

Too strong.

She fought the urge by holding herself rigid in her chair as they went from one seminar to another and listened to various speakers lecture on the latest advances in this or that.

"You're doing well." Marcos glanced up from the notes he'd been jotting on his program during a lull. "You haven't asked for my help. Not even once."

No. Thank God.

"This isn't life or death like at the hospital. If I don't understand a word or two, it won't hurt anything."

"No. I suppose not." He tapped the end of his pen against the program. "But the challenge to understand what's happening around you does make things interesting, yes? What does your family think of you living in another country?"

The sudden change in subject threw her. "They've always encouraged me to think for myself."

The only person who hadn't was gone now. Her fingers curved reflexively into the tops of her legs before she forced them to relax. To lie absolutely flat.

Not wanting to think about her family, she followed his lead. "What about you? Anyone else in your family go into medicine?"

There was a pause, and Maggie thought for a second that her phrasing was off. But then he answered. "My family is a complicated subject. Best left for another time."

Wow. So it was okay for him to ask about her family, but not the other way around. Well, great.

The man burned hot and cold, and she could never predict which one he might be at any given moment. If she felt this way after almost seven months of working with him, she doubted if the next few would bring any serious changes.

He glanced at his watch and swore softly. "It's almost five. Do you mind missing the last session? We need to catch the subway—rush hour in São Paulo is best avoided if at all possible."

"Oh, no, of course not." In actuality, it was a relief to get away. She wasn't sure she understood his hurry, though, since they *had* taken the subway, rather than his car. How would rush hour matter one way or the other if you weren't actually driving?

She soon found out. People getting off work streamed through the turnstiles at the metro station and swarmed down the escalators to reach the lower levels. A faint sense of claustrophobia began to press in around her, and Marcos stopped to take her hand after five or six people came between them, threatening to make her lose sight of him all together.

"You have to be aggressive," he murmured, gripping her fingers and towing her along. "It only gets worse from now until about eight at night."

"Worse?"

He grinned down at her. "Hard to believe, isn't it? But it's exhilarating, no? The life, the movement...the noise."

The noise? No, she found it kind of unsettling. Chaotic. Her instinct was to cling to the railing on the side of the wall and hang on for dear life as the crowds swept around her. She clung to Marcos's hand instead.

And prayed she'd live to see another day.

CHAPTER FIVE

DAMN. HE'D MEANT to leave the conference earlier.

He knew how crowded the *metró* could get at rush hour. Despite how calm she'd seemed during the trip this morning, he could tell Maggie was not enjoying how tightly packed the station was now. Looking at it through the eyes of a foreigner, he could see how it might seem frightening—dangerous even.

Keeping a tight hold on her hand, he forced her to keep up, knowing if he didn't they'd get pushed further and further back, and the conditions behind them would grow worse as rush hour shifted into full swing.

They finally reached the platform, and Marcos eyed the lines, calculating exactly which one would give them the best chance of getting on the next train. Briefcases and purses the size of small suitcases were the norm with passengers. As were boxes and shopping bags. People from all walks of life—and from all socioeconomic levels—relied on public transport, especially on the one day of the week when they were prohibited from driving. His day was Monday. When he'd explained the traffic rotation system to Maggie, she'd stared at him in disbelief. "You mean you're only allowed to drive downtown on four of the five business days? How do people get to work on their off day?"

You made do. Just like he'd done as a kid, when his family hadn't had a car at all...or a game console or even a computer. Just a two-roomed shack in the middle of a *favela*.

And without the license-plate restrictions, what were already snarled traffic conditions in São Paulo would grow even worse.

But it also meant that public transport was busy every single day of the week, because those who couldn't drive rode the bus and subway.

A train whooshed past them, leaving a warm breeze in its wake before pulling to a stop with a drawn-out screech. Gripping her hand once again, Marcos hauled her after him the second the doors opened. They were six stops from their destination, so he headed for the far side of the car to let others board, not even bothering to look for a seat. There would be none at this hour.

And the commuters kept coming—people jamming in all around them. Marcos saw someone jostle Maggie and push past her. She seemed to cringe into herself, edging closer to him. "Come here," he said.

He shifted, turning Maggie around until she gripped the metal pole in front of her, then he bracketed her in, his arms going around her to hold on to the same pole. He then widened his stance a bit to shield her legs with his own. He figured between the solid bar in front of her and him at her back, she would be relatively protected, and he could give her a bit more breathing space than some of the other passengers had.

What he hadn't expected, however, was to feel as if he were holding her in his arms, or the way the back of her head rested against his chest, doing strange things to his insides. She wasn't doing it on purpose, there just wasn't anywhere else for her to go. It also meant her rounded bottom was pressed against his upper thighs.

The doors slid closed and things went from merely uncomfortable to nightmare proportions as the sudden motion of the train pulling away from the platform threw Maggie against him, her body snugging to his in a way that had him spiraling down a dark rabbit hole and putting him on high alert.

"Sorry," she gasped. But every bump and curve in the track had that delectable ass sliding over and into him time and time again.

He'd been trying to protect her. What about protecting himself? Because by the time they got off this train, his situation was going to be very noticeable.

The train began slowing rapidly as it reached its first stop, and Marcos braced one arm on the pole while sliding his other around her waist to keep her anchored against him, and to prevent the people behind him from squeezing Maggie further against the metal bar.

People shifted…some getting off, new passengers crowding closer. Things should get better after the third or fourth stop when they moved further away from the downtown district.

Maggie twisted her head to the side and looked up at him. "Sé Station…isn't this the shopping district? Where I came with Sophia?"

"It is."

The train pulled out again, preventing any further talk as he concentrated on keeping his body under control as the sweet assault from hers continued to grind away at his senses. The clean scent of her hair rose around him, cutting through the other less agreeable smells on the subway, and without realizing what he was doing he pulled it deep into his lungs, leaning closer...until all he smelled was Maggie.

And that's all he felt as well as he leaned into the turns, his arm still wrapped around her, still holding her in place.

Had she just pressed closer?

It had to be his deranged imagination that had her butt nestled between his legs, the small of her back pressing on a very sensitive—and very dangerous—area of his anatomy. And up that area came, right on cue.

Damn.

It was too late to do anything about it now, other than grit his teeth and enjoy the ride.

Except this was one ride that wouldn't be made to completion but would just leave him hungry for more.

Third stop. Three more to go.

If he survived this, he'd need to do some serious penance afterwards. Because his body was howling at him now, and he couldn't help using the momentum of the train to his advantage. He could have sworn that Maggie answered every bump and grind with one of her own.

Marcos closed his eyes. *Just let me make it through this alive.*

Fourth stop.

Maggie's shuddered breath was not his imagination this time. Neither did she move away from him as more people filtered out and fewer people packed on. This should be their cue to start edging away from each other.

He would, when she did. And the woman hadn't budged an inch.

No longer was he praying to make it out alive. He was praying to be dragged down to hell and be done with it.

The train exited the station, and Marcos's hand tightened on her waist once again, his thumb doing an experimental strum down her side. Maggie's knuckles turned white as they gripped the pole in front of her, but there was no hint of struggle or of wanting to get away.

He was doomed.

Fifth stop.

Maggie's blouse had edged up during the trip, and when he shifted his hand, his pinky finger met bare skin. His hard-on was now a raging inferno that showed no hint of subsiding any time soon. And that warm, silky sliver of flesh tempted him to move his hand a little lower, to widen that gap between her trousers and shirt.

He didn't. But his little finger did explore as much as it was able, dragging backwards and then retracing its steps time and time again. He swore he could hear her breath, shallow and rapid above the churning sounds of the train.

Kind of like the churning going on in his gut.

And then the nightmare came to a crashing halt as the train began to slow for the last time...way before he was ready.

He ducked his head low, until his lips almost touched her ear. "This is our stop."

"Is—is it?"

"Yes." Her earlobe was close—a tiny diamond glittering in the delicate flesh. All he had to do was open his mouth and draw it in, stroke his tongue across it.

The subway doors opened with an ugly hissing sound.

Marcos blinked back to awareness as folks around them began moving, exiting with quick, jerky steps, in a hurry to reach their destinations. The fire still burning strong in his belly, he forced himself to take a step back, to unwind his arm from Maggie's waist, pinky making one last desperate pass across her skin before withdrawing completely.

Maggie's shoulders lifted as she let go of the pole. "Ready?"

Not by any stretch of the imagination. But he would take the steps necessary to get off this train.

Both the physical one…and the mental one.

No matter how much he longed to stay.

Except the second he let Maggie move through the open door and followed her off the train, he couldn't draw his eyes away from the soft ass in front of him, or banish the memory of it swishing against him time and time again. And a certain throbbing part of his body made sure that memory stayed painfully alive.

They rounded a corner of the station and exited near a darkened stand of trees. He needed to stop for a second and catch his breath, because if he didn't get control of himself—right now—then the second they reached the parking lot and got into his car, he was going to do something extremely stupid. Like haul her onto his lap, unzip, and put an end to this torture once and for all. He'd done it once before—could remember every second of the time they'd spent doing just that.

Forcing the thoughts back down with a soft curse, he snagged Maggie's hand, tugging her off the sidewalk. People continued to stream by them, oblivious to anything but getting home.

"What—?"

"Shh."

He moved deeper into the bushes, stopping behind a large oak tree. The dark shadows played a tantalizing game of hide and seek with her features.

She blinked at him. "Is something wrong?"

Was she serious?

"Yes, Maggie. Something is terribly wrong." Even as he said it, his back connected with the tree behind him. Taking her other hand in his, he bent his elbows to shift her a few inches closer.

Her tongue came out to dampen her lips, eyes still on his.

She knew. She *had* to know.

Just to make sure, he slid his hands up either side of her neck until his thumbs rested just beneath her chin, applying the barest amount of pressure to tilt her head up. "Can you guess what it is, *querida*?"

"I—I don't..."

"Yes. I think you do." He stared down at her, a strange sense of resignation sliding through him as he realized no place was safe with her. Not a subway, not a car…not even behind a tree. "Come here."

There was a pause then she took one step toward him, then two. Something inside him twisted with a mixture of lust and exultation.

"Do you want me to show you what it is?" he continued, his thumbs caressing the edges of her jawline.

She nodded, then seemed to need to back up the gesture with her voice. "Yes."

The whispered word seemed to unleash something primal in him, and he lowered his head, almost touching her lips. He felt the warmth of her breath as it slid from her lungs in a quick, steady stream in preparation for his kiss. But he wasn't interested in taking her mouth in a rush, like he had in the car. If he was going to kiss her, he was going to make it count—draw it out as long as humanly possible—because Marcos had no idea how long it would be before he tasted those sweet lips again. If ever.

Why wasn't he kissing her? Was he going to back out?

She sensed him close. Had actually shut her eyes in anticipation, but he didn't completely close the gap between them. Parting her eyelids again, she saw he'd stopped less than an inch away, his head tilted at the perfect angle, hovering so close she could have licked his lips if she'd wanted to.

Could have licked his lips...

Before she could think better of it, her tongue came out and touched his full lower lip, then darted back inside her own mouth, quick as a bunny.

Marcos let out a quiet groan that sounded painful. Her heart pounded in her chest as she waited for him to recoil. He didn't. Instead, he muttered something that sounded suspiciously like "Again."

But she wasn't sure. What if he—?

"Again, Maggie." This time there was no mistaking those words.

Slowly, her tongue edged forward and touched him again, this time sliding across that same lip, her eyes closing as the textures she admired each and every day came alive in a completely different way.

His hand slid deep into her hair and held her in place as she explored him. Tracing first his bottom lip, and then moving up to taste the top.

He lifted his head a fraction of an inch until she was at the seam of his mouth, and he opened, his lips surrounding the very tip of her tongue, kissing it softly. The act made her legs wobble beneath her.

She pulled back to swallow and try to catch her breath. She couldn't. The air was long gone from her lungs. Maybe he was some kind of alien creature, and this was his way of sucking the life force out of her. She'd be long dead before she realized what hit her.

Only he made it seem like it was the other way around. That what she was doing was the most exquisite sensation imaginable. He wasn't the only one—touching him gave her chills and heated her up all at the same time.

"Again." His voice was a little hoarser than it had been. "Just once more. And then I'll let you go home."

Let her go home?

She didn't want to go home. Not now. Maybe not ever.

This time when she edged forward, she licked across his lips in a single long swipe, hoping the action came across as sensual and not like a puppy lapping crumbs from his master's hand.

The fingers in her hair tightened just a bit, as if he didn't want to let her go quite yet, despite his words to the contrary. The move emboldened her, and she again approached the seam of his mouth, nudging a bit this time.

It worked. He opened, allowing entry, but her victory was short-lived when he dragged her forward in a rush until she was fully splayed against him—fully aware of every hard inch of his body against hers. His lips finally found hers and all thoughts of coaxing him fled as he swept aside her timid attempts at seduction and replaced them with something that was far removed from anything she could have thought or attempted.

His free hand went to the small of her back and fisted in her shirt, his knuckles grazing bare skin. She gulped back a wave of raw heat when his erection nudged at her belly, just like her tongue had done at his lips seconds earlier. Only this wasn't a request. It was a command. One that she readily answered with a slight tilt of her pelvis—and an inner plea for more of the same. So much more.

"Meu Deus." He dragged his lips from hers, ignoring her squeak of protest and her gripping fingers. "You really are magic—*magía*. You take my noblest intentions and turn them on their head." Pressing his cheek against hers, he drew in a deep breath. "I need to get you home before I forget all the reasons I pulled you back here in the first place."

As he reached for her hand and dragged her back to the realm of reality, rejoining the next wave of travelers as they exited the subway, she couldn't form a single coherent thought or response to what had happened between them.

All she knew was that he'd called her magic. And for a few brief moments...she'd almost believed him.

CHAPTER SIX

"But in the States—"

"You're no longer in the States, Maggie." He made a circle of his forefinger and his thumb as they sat in his car. "And, in my country, this sign is not something you use."

There was a note in his voice—the accented English gruff and bold—that made her shiver. But then again she'd been shivering in his presence for months now. "Why?"

"You don't want to know."

She licked her lips. She did want to know. Desperately. Especially as he'd just shifted his body toward her in his seat, pupils dilating.

"Tell me." The breathy quality to her voice tugged at her, sending a warning that told her to make her way up to the surface. Now. Because danger lay in the direction she was headed.

Not yet. Please. Not yet.

Her water bottle, wet with condensation, slid from her hand and dropped to the console before rolling to the floor by his feet. They both swooped to get it. Cheeks met...slid against each other.

"That sign means something very bad, querida.*"* *One hand went to the nape of her neck, holding her in place as his words continued to whisper past her ear. "So bad, you should never flash it at a patient. Or a man. Unless you want something equally bad to happen to you."*

She swallowed. "Like what?"

He pulled back just far enough that she could see his eyes. The heat swimming in them was sensual. And just a little bit terrifying.

"Like this." His head came down until his lips were inches away, his warm breath washing across her face.

Why did this scene feel so familiar? Like it had already been played out?

His thumb traced a path across the sensitive skin of her neck. "Can you guess what it means now?"

"No." Her breath swept into her lungs, readying itself even before her brain was fully cognizant of what was about to happen.

"Then I must show you, Maggie." His fingers tightened, mouth suddenly sliding across hers with a low groan.

For a split second she couldn't move, couldn't

breathe, an unexpected wave of desire spiraling through her. She froze, eyes blinking wide.

Marcos eased back, a frown on his face. "Meu Deus. *You're frightened.*"

She'd definitely lived through this before. Had heard these exact words—could anticipate his every move. In a past life?

"No. I'm not frightened." It was the truth, because the second his mouth left hers the only thing she was afraid of was that he might not kiss her again.

He stared at her for a long time, before murmuring, "No? Then kiss me back, querida. *And I'll show you exactly what that symbol means."*

Maggie jerked to awareness, her fingers crushing something. His shirt?

She glanced around. No. This wasn't Marcos's car. It was her apartment.

Her bed.

And Marcos had definitely never spent the night in it.

She'd been dreaming. No wonder everything had felt so familiar. Releasing her death grip on the covers, she dragged one of her palms across her face, horrified to find her hand was shaking like a leaf.

He'd shown her what that sign meant all right.

And no matter how much she might deny it during her waking moments, her dreams told a different story. And it was something she was going to have to acknowledge sooner or later.

Far from being over what had happened, she was fixated on it. Enthralled by the memory of his touch.

She'd wanted it on a crowded subway, she'd wanted it as they'd kissed behind that tree.

And she still wanted it—even in her sleep.

She wanted Marcos Pinheiro to show her exactly what "A-okay" meant. Again.

Marcos's phone buzzed in the middle of the seminar, making her jump. A few people seated nearby gave them knowing smiles. Whenever a group of doctors got together, being called away was one of the unavoidable realities of the job. They'd all had it happen at some time or other.

Pulling his smartphone from the holder on his belt, he glanced down at the screen then leaned closer to her. "We need to slide out. There's been a traffic accident."

Following his cue, she got up from her seat, crouching as she tried not to disturb her fellow attendees. By the time she made it to the aisle,

Marcos was halfway to the door, and she had to hurry to catch up.

Not that she wanted to. She'd been struggling to act normally all morning long after waking up swamped by the memory of them together in his car. His scent. His husky words.

The feel of his hands on her hips as he'd directed her movements.

You have a patient. Get it together, Maggie!

Marcos had been his same stoic self, never mentioning what had happened on the subway—or afterwards—although she knew for a fact he was as affected as she was. She'd felt a definite ridge of interest as they'd kissed.

Patient. P-a-t-i-e-n-t. She spelled the word out in her head, using a slow, robotic monotone that she hoped would pop whatever bubble of craziness was floating around inside her.

She caught up with Marcos in the lobby. "What happened?"

"Head trauma. Sixteen-year-old female." A muscle worked in his jaw. "She was a passenger on a motorcycle."

"Oh, no."

The motorcyclists in Brazil took their lives in their hands each and every day, darting back and forth on the heavily traveled roadways and wedging themselves into the most minuscule spaces, or flying down the center line between rows of vehicles with tiny warning beeps of their horns. She'd read somewhere that the average life expectancy of a *motoboy* in São Paulo was thirty-odd years.

"How bad is it?"

Marcos kept walking. "Skull fracture. The driver tried to avoid a man pulling a handcart and plowed into a bus in the neighboring lane. He was killed instantly. The passenger was thrown into one of the concrete road dividers."

Maggie shuddered at the image. "Those handcarts should be outlawed."

His steps faltered for a second before recovering. "People do what they have to do to survive."

"Even if it kills or maims someone else?"

"Have you seen the way those motorcycles drive?" A thread of anger had entered his voice.

"Yes, I've also seen those carts." Piled high with what looked like sacks of garbage, she'd seen men and sometimes boys struggle to keep the rickety contraptions moving, even in rush-hour traffic. Cars were forced to go around them, sometimes having to swerve into the next lane if they came upon one suddenly. Most of the people who pulled those carts lived in the slums that dotted the landscape of São Paulo, a lifestyle so far removed from what she'd known in the States it was hard to fathom.

As if he'd read her thoughts, he said, "It's difficult for the wealthy to understand how the other side lives."

The wealthy? He said it like it was some kind of plague. She'd seen Marcos's car—intimately, in fact—had ridden in it today. He wasn't exactly scraping the bottom of the barrel. And if that "wealthy" crack had been aimed at her, he was sadly mistaken. Her family might have money, but she was still paying her school loans and would be for a long time. It had been a sacrifice to come to Brazil in the first place.

She decided to strike a conciliatory tone. "You're right. It's hard for an outsider like me to understand."

He stopped and turned to face her in the parking lot. "I didn't mean it that way."

Then how *had* he meant it? He acted like he knew from personal experience what it was like to pull one of those carts.

She shook off the thought. Maybe he thought she was insulting his country. If so, she could understand why he might be upset. "It's okay. Do you know anything more about our patient?"

"No. One of my colleagues has ordered a

CT scan. I'll know more once he calls with the results."

As soon as they got in the car, his phone buzzed again. He answered and spoke for a minute or two, before disconnecting and putting the car into gear.

Marcos drove with a surety and confidence that came from years of training, much like the skill with which he performed delicate surgeries that saved lives.

And the skill with which he made love.

A fresh wave of guilt washed over her, and her fingers clutched at the sides of her seat, nails digging into the soft leather. "Was that the other doctor on the phone? What did he say?"

"It doesn't look good. There's bleeding on the patient's brain. They've already had to put her on a ventilator."

Maggie tried to think of the young life that might be tragically altered for ever or, worse, cut short. "Is there any hope?"

"I like to think there's always hope." He slid a glance at her. "It's why I went into medicine."

Interesting. She'd heard so many stories of people becoming doctors for a specific reason, whereas she'd just kind of drifted into it. She'd wanted to help people, but she could have gone in any number of directions to do that. Medicine was just a means to an end.

What she'd really wanted to do was help those who couldn't help themselves.

Because she'd been helpless herself once upon a time?

Probably.

"So that's why you became a doctor? Because you believe in hope?"

"No. Because I believe in keeping my promises."

She looked at him in surprise. "Promises? I don't understand."

"It doesn't matter." He shrugged. "I love what I do. Bottom line, as you would say."

That was his bottom line. He'd become a doctor because of a promise? To whom? His parents? Someone who'd been ill?

"And you became a neurosurgeon because…"

He didn't say anything for a moment or two. "It's hard to verbalize. Let's just say it was something I needed to do. What about you?"

What had made her think she could ask a question like that without him lobbing a similar one back at her? And why did she expect *him* to have an answer when she didn't have one herself?

"I became a doctor to help people. And a neurosurgeon? Maybe to understand how the brain works," she said slowly, wondering if that really might be part of the reason. She'd thought about going into psychiatry before deciding that dealing with emotionally damaged minds might not be the best choice for someone like her. But dealing with physically damaged ones...yes, that she could handle. It was a type of damage she could see. Feel. Do something about without being touched by it herself.

Really?

And what about patients like Teresa Allen? Hadn't the little girl touched her in a way that cut right to her heart?

Maybe, but at least a shunt replacement was something that would definitely fix the child's problem. Unlike her own problem, which even after a couple of years of private counseling— counseling that not even her parents were aware she'd undergone—had still lingered on the fringes of her life, bringing with it the tendency to blame herself for things that were out of her control. Although she was learning to tune out that negative voice.

Like when Marcos had kissed her that first time? Oh, yes. That voice had tried to re-emerge—only to be beaten back. At least she hoped so. Even as she thought it, she became aware of her nails digging into Marcos's expensive leather upholstery again. Appalled, she released her grip on the seat, hoping she hadn't left any permanent marks.

"We're almost there. Do you want to assist? Or would you rather take a taxi back to your apartment?"

"I'm here to learn. I can't do that from my apartment."

He sent her a look that bordered on approval. But something else was mixed in with it. "You sure? Motorcycle accidents aren't pleasant."

"I'm not here for 'pleasant' either."

He pursed his lips. "No. But surely it's not always so bad, is it?"

There was something beneath his words that made her wonder if he was talking about this case or something else. "No. Of course it's not."

He pulled into the parking lot of the hospital and swung around to the underground lot used by staff members, sliding his card into the holder and waiting for the automatic arm to go up. He glanced at his watch as he pulled into the nearest spot. "It's almost five. I have no idea how long this will take."

"It doesn't matter. I'm here until it's finished."

He reached over and squeezed her hand before popping the handle to his door. "Good. Let's go."

Marcos kept his eye trained on the craniotome as it inched along the bony surface of his patient's skull, the saw's eerie whine overriding the saxophone solo from his favorite jazz album each time he engaged the footplate. The background noises around him seeped into his subconscious from time to time, but they didn't distract him. He wasn't sure why it was, but the ebb and flow against his eardrums sharpened his concentration somehow. Some surgeons worked best in a quiet, controlled atmosphere, others—like Marcos—preferred noise. He glanced at Maggie as she studied the images of Stácia Lauro's brain, wondering which type of surgeon she was.

Did she like absolute silence, like when she made love? Were the sounds around her slowly eating away at her composure this very second?

He finished the cut, preparing to lift the section of skull to give the patient's still swelling brain a place to go without herniating through her brainstem. The growing pressure over the past half-hour had thwarted every effort to stall its progress, forcing them to make a life-or-death decision.

"Is the music bothering you?" he asked.

Her gaze still locked on the images in front of her, it took a quarter of a turn of Maggie's head before her eyes shifted to meet his. "I'm sorry?"

"The music. Is it bothering you?" He examined the creamy white section of the patient's exposed dura, frowning at the darkened area where blood had collected beneath the brain's protective cover. Exactly how large was that clot?

"It's fine." She moved toward him to peer down into the open portion of Stácia's brain. "Her motorcycle helmet cracked in half. Her father showed it to me when I talked to him. He's beside himself."

"I know." He closed his eyes for a second. "If the craniectomy does its job and the swelling slows, maybe she'll have a chance. If not…"

He left the words unsaid, but Maggie would know what he meant. They'd have to talk to her devastated parents about organ donation. It was one of the hardest things about his job, even worse than death itself because it involved decisions like artificially keeping someone's body—i.e., their organs—alive, even after there was no hope of regaining brain function. What was a tragedy for one family became a ray of hope for another.

But Marcos wasn't ready to give up on Stácia just yet…as long as she remained stable, they had a shot at preserving cognitive function. And like he'd told Maggie, he wanted to believe there was always hope.

Two hours later, he'd removed the clotted material and did another scan to make sure the brain wasn't bleeding anywhere else.

Suturing the dura and the scalp closed once again, he made a surgical pocket in the patient's abdomen and placed the portion of the skull they'd removed within it. Doing this would keep the bone flap viable for months to come, if necessary—although he hoped it would only be a matter of weeks. If Stácia survived, the bone would be reset in its original spot.

"All we can do at this point is wait." Sweat had collected beneath his surgical gown, despite the chilly temperature in the operating room.

Maggie nodded. "She's lucky to live near a hospital like this one."

He remembered his father, who'd lived not so very far away from this part of the city. "Living near a hospital doesn't always mean much. Some very deserving people never see a doctor."

She blinked at him as if surprised by his answer.

"No. You're right," she said, stripping her gloves off. "And sometimes undeserving people get anything they want."

This time he was the one surprised. "What kinds of things do they get?"

Some dark emotion flashed across her face, and Marcos tilted his head, trying to figure out if she was still talking about medical care or if—like him—she'd shifted to something much more personal.

"Nothing." She gave an almost visible headshake. "I was just thinking out loud. Do you need me for anything else?"

"I think we're about done here. I'm going to stick around the hospital for a couple more hours to see if her condition changes."

"Do you think it will? I could stay as well."

"It's up to you." He wanted to probe a little bit more about those undeserving people, but if it was something she wanted to tell him then she would.

Just like he'd chosen not to say anything about his father.

"I'll keep my cellphone on. Will you give me a call if something happens?"

"If you'd like."

"Thanks. I really would." She tugged her mask up and over her head and discarded it in one of the waste bins. "If not, I'll see you tomorrow. Do you plan to do rounds before the convention?"

"Yes. Around seven-ish."

"Great. I'll see you then."

With that, Maggie reached up to tighten her ponytail and pushed through the door.

And all he could wonder was who those undeserving people Maggie spoke of were…and exactly what they'd gotten.

CHAPTER SEVEN

MAGGIE WAS TALKING to someone.

After stepping outside the convention hall to call the hospital to check on Stácia's condition, Marcos had returned to the lobby to find Maggie engaged in conversation—her animated hand gestures the liveliest he'd seen from her since she'd started working at the hospital. The man she was with nodded at whatever she'd said.

A spike of something strange went through his chest, and he debated whether to let her finish her conversation or make his way over to them.

Stácia was holding her own, the craniectomy finally lowering her intracranial pressure. So there was no immediate danger of her brain herniating. They wouldn't know her long-term prognosis until the swelling went down, however. For now he wanted to keep her in a medically induced coma until she was a little more stable.

Maggie's red hair was a beacon in a sea of dark heads—so he'd spotted her immediately by the counter where water and coffee were being served. And Marcos was tall enough that he was able to see over the crush of people to tell that she was doing a lot of the talking, her face changing with each shift in emotion. She was speaking English. Her mouth movements were quick enough that she was very familiar with her subject matter…wasn't hesitant about choosing her words. He knew a lot of people here, but he didn't know this particular man—although he seemed vaguely familiar. But the smile the guy gave as she responded to something he said was full of interest, his intent eyes never leaving Maggie's face. The man laughed, his hand going up to touch her arm.

That made his decision for him. Marcos veered to the right, rather than heading back through the double doors across the room. By the time he reached her, however, the stranger had handed her something and moved away, but Maggie's eyes followed his progress for another moment or two before swinging around to meet his gaze.

A flash of guilt went through the blue depths before she smiled. Only the smile looked forced, nothing like the carefree grin she'd just bestowed on the good-looking stranger.

And why the hell was he suddenly noticing what other men looked like?

"Who was that?" he found himself asking.

"Oh…um." She licked her lips. "He's a doctor."

He feigned surprise. "No. *Verdade?*"

"Of course it's the truth." Then, as if realizing he was teasing, she added, "He's from my home state."

"He's an American?" Not that people from other nationalities didn't come to these conventions, but it was usually only for specialties in which Brazil excelled.

"Kind of."

His brows went up. "He's *kind of* an American?"

"You know what I mean."

"I really don't." This woman had the power to send his head spinning in all different directions.

"He was born in Brazil but raised in New Jersey. He knows the hospital where I used to work." She seemed to rethink her words. "The hospital where I still work."

The spike that had jabbed his chest pushed a little deeper. "He works at your hospital?"

"No. He practices in California now. But his parents still live in New Jersey. He gave me his card." She handed it to him.

Marcos glanced at the words.

Dr. L. Carvalho. MD FACS
Facial and Reconstructive Surgery
Appointments: 555-555-2389
Cell: 555-555-1930

"He's a plastic surgeon?"

She nodded. "He's here for the conference."

Brazil was a pioneer in that particular area, which explained his presence.

He glanced at Maggie, studying the lines of her face. He could see why a plastic surgeon would gravitate toward someone like her. Her flawless skin and delicate bone structure drew the eye—the dusting of freckles across her nose only adding to her charm. He happened to know from experience those freckles extended to her shoulders. His tongue had nudged aside her shirt as he'd followed the trail a month ago.

Right on cue, his body reacted. On impulse he flipped the card over to the reverse side and saw an email address as well as another phone number scrawled in a messy hand across the back.

"He gave you his private number?"

Maggie's face flushed scarlet. "I came out to the lobby to call my parents—I've been too busy lately to talk with them much. He heard me speaking English and thought we might like to get together for drinks."

I'll bet he did.

He wouldn't ask whether or not she'd agreed to meet him. He settled for something a little less obvious. "You realize there are areas of São Paulo that you shouldn't venture into alone."

"I'm not stupid. I wouldn't knowingly put myself in a dangerous situation."

"No? You don't know this man at all. He could be something other than what he appears."

The tightening of her jaw said she was remembering something. "Sometimes it's not just strangers who aren't what they appear."

Was she talking about him?

He started to respond, just as the doors to the conference hall were pushed closed by two ushers. Maggie nodded in that direction. "I think they're getting ready to begin."

When he started to slide the business card into the pocket of his sports coat, Maggie plucked it out of his hand with an enigmatic smile and dropped it into her purse instead.

Did she really mean to call the man?

It was none of his business. She was probably homesick and hungry for a native English speaker.

He immediately flinched away from the word

hungry, as it called up all kinds of images he'd rather not see. Of Maggie and the dark stranger getting it on in some hotel room—or worse a motel, notorious in Brazil for their hourly rates and clandestine sexual encounters. Maggie might not even know the difference between the two types of establishments.

And that thought made an entirely different image rear its head. Of him—and Maggie—in one of those very motel rooms.

Just before they reached the entrance to the lecture hall, he put his hand on her arm to stop her. "Be careful, okay?"

Marcos wasn't sure if he was warning her off the stranger or off himself.

"Of course I will."

"You don't know anything about this country or what can happen here."

Maggie gave a visible swallow. "You're right. I don't. But I'm quickly finding out."

She'd spoken the truth. She was quickly finding out exactly how dangerous Brazil could be. Not in terms of crime or assaults but in feeling completely out of her league most of the time with her boss.

She'd been so grateful to find someone to talk to

who was open…whose body language she could read without second-guessing every little nuance. Unlike the brooding doctor who sat beside her—who she couldn't read if her life depended on it.

He was gorgeous…just as handsome as the doctor she'd spoken to in the lobby. But whereas she found herself over-thinking everything Marcos said or did, the stranger she'd met was easy to decipher—his face withholding nothing and revealing everything. Even the hint of interest, which had given her a surge of confidence.

It would serve Marcos right if she did call him.

Really? Other than warning her of potential danger, he didn't act like it would matter one way or the other to him.

They'd slept together, and he'd kissed her behind the trees at the subway station…so he found her physically attractive, but then again she'd been in that kind of situation before. Someone had found her attractive in the past and had taken what he'd wanted.

No, that wasn't fair.

Marcos hadn't taken anything she hadn't freely given. In fact, she felt safer with him than she had with any other man, even the casual boyfriend she'd had a couple of years ago. While she'd finally learned that sex could be an enjoyable experience, rather than something to be dreaded, her body's reaction to Marcos had been completely unexpected—shattering her lukewarm expectations and haunting her dreams. She wanted more of the same, even though it was out of the question. Those cravings—for her boss, of all things—had reawakened a guilt she'd thought long gone.

But it was obvious he wasn't interested in anything other than her body. To all appearances, he'd taken what had happened between them in his stride, never missing a beat. Neither had he apologized for what had happened in his car or on the subway. Maybe it wasn't as out of the ordinary for him as it was for her.

Did she really want him to apologize? Wouldn't that be the ultimate slap in the face?

She had no idea.

She only knew that if you could have too much of a good thing, then a few days of a not-so-good thing could quickly turn into pure torture.

Seated next to Marcos, she'd finally decided that was the best term to describe her current situation: torture. It had taken her four days to realize that what she'd hoped would be a reprieve in their uneasy working relationship was actually the opposite. No, they hadn't ridden the subway again—and Maggie honestly didn't know what she was going to do when Monday rolled around and they found themselves back on it. Because, even sitting quietly in the convention hall, she was aware of exactly how many millimeters separated her knee from Marcos's, and it was driving her crazy.

Because the space was always way too small.

She whispered a question about their patient, and Marcos leaned over to fill her in, his breath smelling of coffee and the mint he'd evidently consumed some time afterwards. Goose bumps rose along the side of her neck, and Marcos must have noticed because he pulled back a few inches to tell her the rest.

Which sent a stream of crushing humiliation pumping through her veins. Why did her body have to be so obvious about sending out signals? Why couldn't she be more like her boss…cool, calm, and supremely unflappable.

Except on the subway, and then again afterwards when she'd felt the very obvious reaction to their proximity.

But surely that had been a guy-mashed-against-girl thing. Her response hadn't been any better, but she could blame it on the same thing. He was an attractive man, and he'd wanted her. For a few minutes anyway.

The only reprieve to their time at the conference

lay in the fact that their patient was still not out of the woods, and Marcos had been cutting their days shorter in order to go back to check on her.

None of that helped.

Because she swore Marcos could see inside of her. Like when she'd talked about people not always being who they appeared to be.

The words had come out before she'd really thought about them.

The situation with her uncle wasn't something she wanted Marcos to discover. It had been a soul-crushing time in her life that she didn't like revisiting. Looking back on it now, she knew it was wrong not to have told her parents or her aunt… she would never in a million years counsel another child to remain silent in the face of something so horrific.

But she'd been a child herself. If someone had asked her outright what was going on behind their backs, would she have spoken up?

Maybe. But no one would have ever guessed Uncle Ted was not a loving, kind husband who'd lavished affection on everyone in the family.

And especially on his "favorite" niece.

She'd avoided him when she'd been able to.

And when she hadn't, she'd paid the price.

It made her realize Marcos was right about trusting strangers. She needed to be smart. Careful. Maybe she should chuck Dr. Carvalho's business card in the trash when she got home. Except she'd also given him her Brazilian cellphone number. That had been stupid of her. What if he actually called and asked her to go out?

She could just say no. Tell him she was busy.

After all she was, most days. And she'd learned not to let anyone walk all over her again. *Stop means stop*, as her therapist had been so fond of saying.

So why hadn't she said it to Marcos that day in the car? Because the last thing she'd wanted had been for him to stop.

"Are you okay?" His voice pulled her from her thoughts, a thread of worry in his tone.

She blinked and glanced down to where her fingernails were digging into the soft flesh of her thighs through her slacks—the pain both old and familiar. The urge to welcome it back slid over her.

Do it. You'll feel better. You know you will.

She released the pressure instead. Her therapist had said the compulsion—forged over many years—wouldn't magically disappear. It would lurk, like an addiction, hoping to tempt her back into old habits. The trick was to avoid anything that could act like a trigger.

Did that mean Marcos?

Speaking of Marcos, she realized he was still waiting for an answer. "I'm fine. Just a little tired."

Tired of being on edge. Tired of this hyper-awareness of each breath the man beside her drew. Tired of second-guessing every decision she made.

"We can leave after this seminar, if you want."

Relief poured over her in a flood. "Would you mind terribly?" she whispered back.

He shook his head. "I want to check on our patient anyway."

Perfect. That would give her a chance to clear her head and figure out exactly what she needed to do to get through the next four months—until her time in Brazil was over and done.

She stared down at her splayed hands, where thin crescents of white showed above the tops of her nail beds. She could start by cropping those back to their customary nubs so there was no opportunity to revert to destructive behaviors of the past.

Then she could stay far, far away from any kind of temptation, both new and old.

She avoided glancing at the man next to her.

And maybe this time she could actually stick to that plan.

CHAPTER EIGHT

WHAT THE HELL had she been doing to herself?

He pressed the button on the water cooler in his apartment, letting the icy liquid fill his glass. He downed it with several long gulps, the chill hitting his stomach and helping to ground him back in reality.

Because what he'd witnessed this afternoon had been a study in the surreal.

For the last fifteen minutes of the conference he'd watched as Maggie had methodically pressed her nails deep into her thighs and then pulled them back, the action reminding him of a cat extending and retracting its claws. But this had a strange quality to it—the sight casting a shadow of uneasiness over him that had been hard to dispel.

He'd wondered if she'd been in pain for a minute or two—a headache, menstrual cramps, or something like that.

The second he'd asked if she was all right, however, she'd given a violent start and stared down at her lap as if horrified. She'd carefully uncurled her fingers and laid her palms across her legs, keeping them perfectly flat. She'd gone back to being the still, silent figure he'd grown accustomed to.

But below the surface?

If he could peek at the pale skin beneath her slacks, he knew exactly what he'd find. Ugly red welts dotting the surface of her flesh.

It suddenly made him wonder what other parts of Maggie were covered in welts. Not the areas you could see, but the parts you couldn't.

He set his glass down on the marble countertop and wandered aimlessly around his living room as he tried to think through the possibilities. He should have been asleep hours ago, but he couldn't shake the feeling that something was wrong—and hoping he wasn't the cause.

He'd been domineering when he'd crushed her mouth at the subway station. Maybe she really was afraid of him. But she'd seemed to want his kiss just as badly as he'd wanted hers.

Making his way over to a cabinet against the wall, he stopped in front of a large flatscreen television. A small ornate frame was propped next to it, the sizes between the two a study in contrasts. He picked up the picture and stared at the faded, ragged image beneath the glass. It was the only picture he had of his family. His mother held Lucas, who was still a baby, as she sat on the empty handcart at the top of their street, while his father gripped the front pull bar. He himself stood beside the cart, hands on his hips as if he were king of the world. He remembered the day. He'd been happy—so proud of their few possessions. He cringed as he thought back on it.

He couldn't imagine his parents having the money to buy a camera, so the photo had to have been taken by tourists or someone with enough resources to both take the picture and have it printed.

He was glad whoever had snapped the shot had given them a copy. It was the only physical thing he had of all of them together.

For the millionth time he wondered what had happened to his brother. It was possible that he himself was the only surviving member of his family.

The loneliness that swept over him seemed to amplify the silence around him. Setting the picture down, he scooped up the remote to his television and switched it on, turning the sound up enough to drown out whatever stupid emotions were welling up within him.

All because of Maggie and that blank, desolate

stare as she'd dug her nails into her legs time and time again. What kind of pain made a person act like that?

He stared at the remote in his hand as the sounds of raucous, canned laughter from a pre-recorded show surrounded him and he wondered if maybe he and Maggie weren't so very different after all.

Twice.

The number of times Maggie had seen the handsome stranger loitering in the lobby of the conference center since their initial meeting. And the number of times she'd ducked through another set of doors undetected.

They'd just started their second week of the conference, but they'd had to skip out of today's sessions. The swelling in Stácia's brain was subsiding, a mere six days after the accident—which was almost unheard of. Marcos wanted to reattach the bone flap they'd removed as soon as it was feasible to reduce the risk of infection.

She pulled her hands from beneath the faucet, having already scrubbed up for the surgery.

As she prepared to slide her fingers into the gloves, she glanced at her nails, which were now chopped back to nothing, just the way she liked them. Even if they misbehaved the next time she was at the conference—or, worse, at the ballet two days from now—they'd find themselves without traction.

As if they had minds of their own.

No. It was all her. It always had been.

Her nails—long and sharp during those terrible days—had been one way to maintain rigid silence. A way to scream without anyone hearing. The searing pain she'd inflicted on herself had also provided a way to focus on something of *her* choosing. Not his.

And he'd wanted her full attention.

His death of a heart attack during a business trip had put an end to the abuse, but it hadn't put an end to her compulsion. The endorphins released every time she hurt herself brought about a wave of calm during stressful times. But it had also been destructive to both body and soul.

Her therapist had helped her find positive strategies to cope with her fears and frustrations when they came up. It had been several years since she'd actively scratched herself, the sunken white scars the only reminder of what she'd once done.

So why was that familiar tingle raising its ugly head again?

Maybe it was Marcos's comments about not everyone being safe…or that vague warning about what could happen in São Paulo. It made things from the past rush back to mind.

Or maybe it was guilt over her growing feelings for Marcos, and how little control she seemed to have over them. Was her subconscious trying to block out the attraction by shifting her focus to something else?

That had to be it.

Finally ready to join the surgical team, she exited the scrub room and pushed through the doors of the operating room, where she found Marcos examining the area on Stácia's abdomen where he'd stored the bone flap.

She kept her fingers flexed and relaxed as she approached the table. "I'm here."

He glanced to the side, eyes searching her face for a second or two. "Just getting ready to make the incision. The EEG shows an increase in brain activity, so that's an encouraging sign."

"I hope so."

"The plan is to start weaning her off some of the meds and let her slowly regain consciousness. We're not out of the woods yet, though."

No they weren't. Because that strange sensation that happened whenever she was around Marcos was still there. As strong as ever.

He made the cut just above the incision from the

last surgery, and retrieved the bone, examining it carefully through his surgical loupes as a second doctor closed the incision. He glanced at her over the tops of the magnifying lenses. "Looks good. I don't see any areas of bone resorption, although I didn't expect any after this short length of time."

"I'm surprised the swelling went down so quickly."

"I am as well, but I'm not about to complain." He sluiced the bone flap with sterile saline solution and moved up to Stácia's head, where a tray of tools was already in place. "Have you done one of these before?"

"I have. Twice. Decompressive craniectomies at my hospital back home are usually reserved for cases where there's an imminent threat of death, though."

"Yes, they are here as well." His movements were deft as he reopened the site on Stácia's head and then matched the edges of the bone flap, using a combination of wire and screws to secure it in place. Even through the latex gloves, his fingers were lean and strong as they reconstructed the patient's skull. Cosmetically, the work would be undetectable once everything healed. Maggie could only pray the damage to the soft tissues of the brain would be just as unnoticeable.

Unlike the damage once inflicted on her own body and mind?

But just like their patient, the damage couldn't be seen on the outside—for the most part anyway.

Except for what she'd done to herself.

No, she looked like any other woman who'd had a healthy and happy childhood. But deep inside, there were scars that would never disappear. Just like those blemishes on the outsides of her thighs, where she'd gouged at her own flesh. Those tiny marks were just the tip of the iceberg, warning anyone she might get involved with that there were worse things hidden under the surface.

Danger! Keep away!

Her boyfriend had been repelled by them, although he'd done his best to hide his reaction. If Maggie was honest, he'd probably been more horrified by what they represented—although she'd never told him everything that had happened. His subtle avoidance of the tops of her legs when they'd made love had made her feel self-conscious, the feeling growing over the months they'd been together. When she'd finally broken things off, he'd seemed more relieved than anything.

She'd been leery of opening herself up like that again. Marcos hadn't been able to see the scars when they'd come together, and for that she was grateful. The last thing she wanted to do was to explain them to him and watch his eyes grow dark with disgust over what had happened to her. Over what she'd done as a result of it.

For some reason, what he thought about her mattered. A lot.

The rest of the surgery was uneventful, and Maggie was relieved to get out of there. She had a date with Sophia this afternoon to choose their dresses for the ballet. The outing would give her some time to decompress and get away from Marcos.

Physically away, that was. Because it was much harder to flee her thoughts. Thoughts that, for some reason, all seemed to revolve around the one person she needed to forget.

"This is the one. You have to get it!" Sophia made her turn around one more time before pulling her over to the mirror on the side wall of the tiny boutique. Standing behind her, her friend draped her arms around Maggie's neck, her impish face appearing just over her shoulder. "Just look at yourself. You're gorgeous."

Maggie twisted her lips in amusement over the other woman's enthusiasm, but did as Sophia asked. Silky green fabric shimmered as it floated down her figure until it reached her hips, where side gathers emphasized her narrow curves, making them appear more generous than they actually were. There were no shoulder straps to the thing, and Maggie tugged the bodice up with a worried frown. "Are you sure this won't fall down in the middle of the ballet?"

Sophia let go of her and moved around to the front to look.

The salesperson, who was hovering nearby, stepped forward and took hold of the back of the dress, doing something that snugged it tight against Maggie's breasts, making the tops of them spill slightly over the upper edge of the dress. "Better, yes?"

Better if you were intent on putting your assets on full display—which was something she never did. But Maggie had to admit the floaty fabric and jeweled tone did make her look better than she normally did. But wasn't that considered false advertising?

No, because she wasn't advertising anything. To anyone.

"Yes, but I don't sew," she said, hoping that would be that and that they'd put her in something beige with long sleeves and a high neckline. Something that would make her invisible.

"No need. Our seamstress can alter it to fit." The woman smiled at her, obviously not deterred in the least.

Maggie tried again. "You have a *costureira* here at the store?"

Sophia laughed. "Of course they do. Most dress shops do alterations. And you must get this dress. Marcos will love it. His jaw will hit the floor when he sees you."

The last thing she wanted was for anyone's jaw to drop, or for her friend to get the wrong idea. "Marcos isn't interested in how I dress."

"*Verdade?* I've seen the way he looks at you from time to time. He likes you. I can tell."

Like was not the right word. They'd had sex *once*, for heaven's sake—it was called lust. Or insanity. Besides, what Sophia'd probably seen had been embarrassment. Or annoyance that the Master of Control had deigned to give in to a momentary rush of hormones. Maggie was just as guilty of giving in to her urges. Her follicle-stimulating hormone was obviously functioning at optimal levels.

None of that meant she or Marcos liked each other.

Liar. What about the bump and grind on the subway? That crazy kiss afterwards?

They'd been caught up in the moment. It still meant nothing. And all it had done was make things more awkward than ever.

The salesperson, probably knowing when it was smart to slide away, murmured something about going to get the seamstress and that she'd be right back.

"Sophia, he doesn't look at me any differently than he does any other member of the staff. Or you, for that matter."

"Me?" She laughed. "Oh, no. Marcos and I are like brother and sister. The orphanage was so big we learned to stick together at an early age. I kind of adopted him."

Only one word in Sophia's entire speech stood out.

"Orphanage?" she asked.

"Well, yes. That's where we lived." Sophia's brows arched. "He didn't tell you?"

"That he grew up in an orphanage? No."

Her friend bit the corner of her lip, obviously trying to figure out how to say something. "Marcos, his brother and I lived there together. Only Marcos's brother…" She paused. "I think it is better if he tells you himself. I'm sorry, Maggie. I thought you already knew. This won't make you think badly of him, will it? That he was a *moleque*?"

Maggie made a pretense of casually adjusting the dress, but her mind was reeling over the word Sophia had used. Marcos Pinheiro had once been a street urchin? He'd lived in an orphanage? She could have sworn he'd come from a wealthy background. He was urbane, self-confident and practically oozed sophistication. That sophistication had been part of why she'd fallen for him so hard—he knew exactly what to say, what to do, to leave her panting for more. Nothing like she'd expect of someone who'd lost the people he'd loved most. And he had a brother!

She stopped fiddling and laid her hand on Sophia's arm, glancing to make sure the salesperson was still out of earshot. "Of course it won't make me think badly of him."

It actually made her admire him even more. Maybe he wasn't as impervious as he seemed. Maybe he had vulnerabilities he hid from the world, just like she did. Her fingers curled in for a second, her nails touching her palms before she forced her hands back open. Had he ever had anything precious ripped from him?

His parents, obviously—although Sophia didn't mention them at all. And he'd never mentioned a brother. It was on the tip of her tongue to ask, but it didn't feel right to do so. Especially as Sophia had pulled back suddenly, as if she'd said something she hadn't intended to. Even now her hands were twined together, knuckles white.

Time to put her mind at ease. And what would it hurt if Marcos's jaw really did hit the floor? Not that it would. But the slight prodding inside her to try made her decision.

"Well, I think I'm in love with this dress. Are you sure you don't need one?"

Sophia's shoulders relaxed, and she shook her head. "I've been a bridesmaid often enough that I have more than my share of formalwear." Something about the way she said it sounded wistful. But before Maggie had time to dwell on it, her friend went on, "Let's have them put a rush on the alterations and then go and make our nail and hair appointments."

Nails and hair? Maggie winced. Her nails had practically been hacked off to the quick—out of necessity, rather than efficiency. Besides, getting dolled up wasn't one of those things she particularly relished. But Sophia was on a roll. And knowing she'd been an orphan made her friend's happy enthusiasm over the smallest of things seem that much more understandable. It was also why she seemed younger than she probably was.

And Maggie had a feeling that not much deterred the other woman when she had her mind set on something.

But as long as those ideas didn't have anything to do with her and Marcos, she should be just fine.

CHAPTER NINE

MARCOS PRESSED THE intercom on Maggie's apartment building, sending a quick glare at the car on the other side of the street.

Why was Sophia being so stubborn? He would have preferred her to sit in the front seat with him, but she'd insisted that Maggie was a guest.

She was no guest. What she was was an enigma, an expert at getting under his skin and staying there, before proceeding to drive him crazy with need.

Magic.

More like a voodoo sorceress who chanted incantations every night in an effort to make his blood boil and his gut ache. Whatever it was, it worked. He was under her spell, the last place he wanted to be.

The doorman answered, and he glanced at the paper in his hand. "Apartment 203."

A minute later Maggie's voice floated through

the speaker. "I'm almost…um…" A weird pause. "Is Sophia there, by any chance?"

He rubbed the back of his neck. "She's waiting in the car."

"I'm having a slight problem. Could you ask her to come up?"

His regrets about agreeing to go with them grew. Why hadn't he just booked a patient for tonight and played the forgetfulness card? He slid a finger behind the constricting band of his bow-tie and tried to ease the growing pressure. "Maggie, she's in the parking lot across the street. Is it something I can help with?"

He glanced at the steady row of traffic between him and the car lot. It had taken for ever for the light to change when he'd crossed over here. He spied Sophia looking at him, and he held up a finger to let her know it would be another minute.

"No… I mean, that's okay. I'll ask my doorman to help."

Visions of Maggie with a zipper stuck halfway up that creamy back made him swallow hard. No way in hell did he want a doorman helping her with anything.

Although why it mattered was still beyond him. "Let me come up."

She didn't say anything, and he thought for a

moment she might refuse, but then the sound of the front-door buzzer had him pushing through the entrance. The *porteiro* turned a guestbook toward him, and Marcos scribbled his name, the time, and Maggie's apartment number in the appropriate spaces. At least she'd chosen a secure building.

He got into the elevator, punching the button for her floor. He'd been counting on facing Maggie with Sophia in tow. Maybe he should have just gone back to get her.

Too late now.

The elevator doors opened, and he exited, crossing to ring the bell at the appropriate apartment. Before he could do so, the door swung open, and Maggie stood there, a pair of silver shoes in her hands.

"Hi."

For a few seconds his mind refused to function, and he gathered from the fact that he was breathing through his mouth that it was hanging wide open.

He snapped it shut. "Hi."

Maggie had on a dress that should have been illegal. There wasn't a damn thing covering her naked shoulders, and as his eyes trailed down to where the dress hugged her torso, he could see the tops of her breasts. Also naked.

Not her whole breasts…but enough to set loose a series of X-rated images in his skull.

Yes, Brazilian women dressed like this all the time. And, yes, it was part of his culture, he should be used to it.

But something about seeing Maggie—who'd always covered up everything except those fantastic calves—standing there like that caused those voodoo-doll pricking sensations to erupt over his entire body. "You have a problem?"

Mouth-breathing again. Hell. He ground his teeth together and locked his jaws tight.

She held out the shoes. "Sophia loaned me these, but…" she licked her lips. "All the straps… Every time I try to stick my foot in, it's the wrong way."

He saw immediately what the problem was. There was a tangled crisscrossing of thin silver bands on the top of the shoe. So many that it wasn't at all obvious where her foot should slide through. And the buckle and latch were set on opposing diagonals, one at the top, the other at the bottom. She was right. It was a mess.

"Maybe I should just walk to the car barefoot and have Sophia show me how it's done."

Like Cinderella fleeing from the ball? He didn't think so.

The ludicrousness of the situation hit him as they both stood there staring at the sandals, and he couldn't hold back a soft chuckle. "We're both brain surgeons, Maggie. How hard could it be?"

She grinned back. "Pretty hard. I think whoever designed these had a degree in engineering."

"Sit down for a minute, and let me see if I can figure it out."

"I've already tried, and Sophia is probably wondering where we are."

"She knows I've come up." His brows lifted in question. "Afraid I'll be able to figure it out when you couldn't?"

"Of course not." She spun around to walk toward the living room, and Marcos thought his eyes might bug out of his head. He'd assumed the dress wrapped tightly around her entire body, kind of like a towel, with a single panel of green fabric. No. That would be far too easy.

This monstrosity had two wide satin straps that crossed at the back, running from where they were attached at the top of the dress to a point on the opposite side about six inches down. It held the dress up in front, but the straps formed a wide V at the back. And below those straps? Nothing. Not until you reached the small of her back—where the slinky fabric cupped her bottom in a way that made his mouth water. The same butt he'd lusted over since that day on the subway.

This was just great.

She glanced over her shoulder. "Coming?" He swore there was the slightest hint of a smile on her lips.

"Not yet. But I'm close." He muttered the words to himself, hoping she hadn't heard him.

Once she sat down, he'd be fine, right?

Maggie perched on the edge of a brown leather sofa and a slender foot appeared from beneath the dress. She handed him one of the shoes.

Cinderella, part two. Wasn't this what he'd been trying to avoid? Images of her in that role with him kneeling beside her as Prince Charming?

Except he was much more likely to be cast in the role of pauper with Maggie as the royal princess, considering their respective backgrounds.

He knelt beside her, and she frowned.

"No, wait. I just wanted you to help me figure out where I'm supposed to shove my foot."

He couldn't hold back another smile. "I'm sure you could think of a few places."

Her lips twisted as if she was fighting her own smile. "Here, give it to me. I'll do it."

Keeping hold of it, he glanced up at her. "I thought you already tried."

"I have."

"Then let me see if I can figure it out. Sometimes it just takes a fresh pair of eyes."

How hard could it be? He'd done this in reverse many times in the past. Yes, but he'd never actually helped a woman get back *into* her shoes before.

Then again, he and Maggie seemed to do everything backwards.

"See why I wanted Sophia? They're her shoes."

He didn't answer, setting the object on the floor and studying it. He matched up straps with the proper side of the shoe, just like he'd do when piecing together a bone flap, like the one he'd reattached to Stácia Lauro.

There were four points where the straps crossed in the middle. He set those together. A tiny diamond buckle sat at the lower right hand side of the shoe, while the strap with the holes was at the top left, so it had to go over the whole mass like so. He slid the end through the buckle just to keep it straight. And this last loop with elastic at the back… He tested the length. Too short for her foot to fit through it, so it must go around the back of her heel.

He undid the buckle then carefully turned the shoe around, lifting the crazy bunch of straps up and away to create a pocket, while leaving the back loop alone. "Okay, slide your foot underneath my hand and see if this works."

Maggie held her foot up and tilted it forward. It whispered into the shoe on the first try—glittery silver toenails winking up at him as they passed through the labyrinth and came to a stop at the end of the shoe.

Success!

He tugged the back loop up over the curve of her heel until it settled in the tiny arch where the back of her foot met her ankle. "I think we got it."

Taking the loose strap, he inserted it into the buckle and pulled it snug. "How's that?"

"Wow. You're quite the expert when it comes to women's shoes."

The words had a strange sound to them, and he eyed her, wondering if she was referring to he and Sophia being more than friends. But he didn't think that was it. The word *women* was plural.

He wasn't going to deny it. He'd had his share of female companionship. But they'd all been willing, and they'd all known where things had stood when the night was over. Which was nowhere.

No promises made. No promises broken. Ever.

Better to keep his responses light. "Brain surgeon. Remember?"

"I do remember."

The words were still tight-sounding. Hell, this was ridiculous. "Give me the other shoe, and I'll set it up for you."

The handoff was made in silence. Now that he'd done it once, Marcos made short work of untangling the straps and putting them in the right order. He handed the shoe back to her.

Maggie slipped it on and leaned over to buckle the thing, the front of her dress gaping a bit and giving him a nice view of pale skin and the soft creamy mounds of her... He stood to his feet in a rush.

When she straightened, holding her dress up to wiggle both her feet, she bit her lip. "People actually walk in these?"

Brazilian women loved their towering heels. They wore them with everything, including jeans. "Don't ask me how. Straps I can do. Surgery I can do. The mystery of the high heel, however, still eludes me."

She stood and drew in a deep breath, the top of her head now reaching his chin. "I couldn't get them on to practice walking in them. Good thing we don't have to take the subway."

Sudden color bloomed in her cheeks and silence filled the room as they stared at each other. Marcos remembered every painful second of that subway ride. And with those heels on, that would put her ass right on a level with a certain worrisome area of his body.

He turned away before he could dwell on that thought. "Sophia is probably wondering what's happened to us, so if you're ready…"

"I am." He heard a clinking sound behind him and glanced back in time to see her pick up a silver purse with metallic links making up the shoulder strap. She followed him to the door.

"Don't you need a sweater…" he gestured in the general direction of her top "…or something?"

"Nope. No sweater."

Just bare shoulders. And shoes that he now knew how to operate.

A deadly combination that he was going to regret at some point this evening.

His only salvation was that Sophia was serving as chaperone. And right now he could bow down at the woman's feet and worship the ground she walked on. Because she was going to save him a whole lot of grief.

CHAPTER TEN

"I DON'T FEEL WELL."

Maggie turned to glance at her friend in concern as they stood in the lobby during intermission. Sophia had been fanning herself almost nonstop during the entire first half of the ballet. It was freezing in the arts center, but that hadn't stopped the other woman from swishing her program back and forth near her face.

In reality, the rhythmic movement had helped keep Maggie's mind busy and off the tuxedo-clad man who'd been seated beside her.

Marcos had taken her breath away when she'd opened the door to find him standing there, his black suit and impeccable white shirt setting off the tanned skin just above his collar. His hair had still been damp, and he'd smelled of soap with a hint of spicy aftershave, which had swirled around her senses, rendering her speechless. He'd seemed pretty shocked himself, although his jaw hadn't quite hit the floor, like Sophia had promised it would. When she'd turned around, though, she had heard his breath hissing in through his teeth.

Right now, he was off talking to another suited man, who'd waved him over almost as soon as they'd come through the doors. Marcos seemed to know pretty much everyone. Considering how huge São Paulo was, that was saying a lot.

Her eyes fastened on Sophia's face. "Do you want to go home?"

"I think I do. Would you mind terribly?"

"Of course not. I'll just tell Marcos we need to leave."

She shook her head. "No. You should both stay and enjoy the rest of the ballet."

What? No!

"If you think I'm going to let you go home by yourself, you're wrong. What if you pass out or something?"

"It's just a headache. I get them sometimes. I'll be fine as soon as I get home and take a cool shower."

"Marcos won't—"

"*Pfft*. He's like an old man. He worries all the time." She touched Maggie's hand. "The subway is right across the street. I'll text you the second I get on the train and when I get back to my apartment, okay? There are *policia* right outside the door, see?"

She motioned at the open door, where there were indeed two uniformed officers, one on either side of the street. And Maggie could see the subway station not two hundred yards away, with people going to and from the well-lit entrance.

"I'll text you," Sophia repeated. "If you don't get one when I get on the train, you can send Marcos to the rescue. It's his favorite role, you know: protector. He drove me crazy when we were kids."

Maggie bit her lip, still unsure. She glanced out the door again and saw the same officers. "Text me."

"I will. Promise." Then with a quick smile that looked suspiciously headache-free, she flounced through the doors and headed toward the street, pausing to toss her program into the trash can at the edge of the sidewalk. She waved to one of the officers as he stopped traffic to let her pass.

Turning back around, Maggie squeaked when she met dark brown eyes, double furrows marring the space between his brows. "Where's Sophia?"

"She...um..." She blinked, wondering what exactly she could say. "She left."

He cocked his head. "Left to go where, exactly?"

She wished she could smirk at him and say the

other woman had just gone to the restroom and that he should cool it. Instead, she found herself wondering if she was about to become the object of his wrath. "She had a headache. She went home."

"And you just let her go?" Each word came across as an accusation, although Maggie had a feeling it was more out of worry for Sophia's safety than anything.

"No, of course not. I tried to tell her I would get you, but she called you an old man." She turned her head. "There are policemen right there, see?" She parroted Sophia's words, knowing she was babbling, but she couldn't seem to stop herself.

Just then her purse vibrated. She clicked it open with shaking fingers and pulled out her phone.

On train. see? safe & sound. txt u when arrv.

She turned the screen to face Marcos. "She's on the train. She's promised to let me know when she gets home."

"So I see." One side of his mouth lifted in something resembling a smile, although she supposed if she tilted her head just right, it might look more like a snarl. "Did you two cook this up?"

Okay, maybe it wasn't a smile… "Cook what up?"

"This…" He swirled his hand around, sweeping it from her face to about hip level. "This whole evening, with the shoes, and dress, and Sophia's sudden departure."

Her eyes widened as she realized where this was headed. He thought she and Sophia had gotten together and planned some kind of seduction scene? Right. He'd already seen how good she was at that. If anyone was the expert, it was him.

"No. We didn't." Her mouth tightened as a wash of anger went over her. The nerve of the man. "And I'd be just as happy to skip the rest of the evening, if it's all the same to you."

Her phone buzzed again. She peered at the screen. "'Sé station.' She knew you'd be worried, so she's probably going to count down every single stop along the way."

A slow infusion of color went up his neck, making the stiff collar of his shirt seem even whiter. "I know firsthand how much good that does."

"I'm sorry?"

"Nothing." He smiled, the furrows easing just as suddenly as they'd come. "How are your feet?"

"Killing me." She risked a smile in return. "Any other questions?"

He nodded. "How interested are you in seeing

this particular ballet? Because I know a little place where we could get a bite to eat, and you could lose those shoes."

"This is so beautiful." Maggie dug her bare toes into the still warm sand beneath her chair and took a sip of her wine.

Moonlight glimmered off the water, casting a crescent of light that seemed to go on for ever. And every time she drew a breath, the heavy scent of the sea rushed in to fill her lungs before drifting away again. Just like the waves.

Marcos swirled the wine in his own glass and looked off into the distance. "I thought you might like it."

"I love it. Thank you for suggesting it." She sighed. "It's hard to believe it's winter in the States right now. But the water is chilly in New Jersey, even in the summer."

"You've lived there your whole life?"

"Yes. My parents were from there, as were their families." Everyone except her uncle, who'd found little things to complain about constantly— even while laughing his words off as jokes. Like the time he'd made fun of her haircut when she was ten, saying it made her look like a boy. He'd chuckled and nudged her arm as if he'd found the whole thing hilarious. Four years later, the joke had been on her. If she'd known when she was ten what she'd learned as a teenager, she'd have kept her hair cropped short—tried to really make herself look like a boy rather than a girl who'd developed earlier than everyone else in her class. And had gained her uncle's attention in an entirely different way.

A deep sliver of pain went through her right thigh, calming her almost instantly. She closed her eyes and took it in.

"Why do you do that?"

Maggie turned her head to glance at him. "Do what?"

He nodded at her lap, drawing her attention to the nails she'd dug into the top of her leg.

Her breath whooshed out of her lungs as she tried to stem the panic and desperation that raced through her veins. She'd stupidly let Sophia talk her into getting acrylic nails for the event—not long ones, but long enough evidently to score some points with her subconscious. Sophia had tsked and clucked over the terrible state of her natural nails, having no idea that she cut them down to nubs on purpose.

Smoothing her dress back down over her thighs, she tried to wipe away the visible imprints she'd left on the shiny fabric. "It's nothing. Just a nervous habit. An *old* nervous habit."

"Talking about your family makes you nervous?" His lips thinned. "Or is it me?"

She tried to evade the question. "I'm not used to having long nails. I keep them cut short because of my job."

"But they used to be long. Or the habit would not have developed." He set down his wineglass and picked up her free hand, examining it. "Very pretty. This is Sophia's doing, I take it."

The man was more intuitive than she gave him credit for. On more than one level. And that meant she needed to be very careful. She tugged her hand back, took a quick slug of wine and decided to address his second statement while ignoring the first. "Sophia's very persistent."

"She is. That persistence used to get her into trouble at times." He ran his thumb over his lower lip as if thinking, an act that reminded her that she'd swept her tongue across that very same lip not that long ago. "So, if it's an *old* habit, and you keep those nails short now, something must have triggered it. I wonder what."

The word "trigger" made her freeze for a couple of seconds before she realized he was using it in a general sense and not as a psychological term. It had been one of her therapist's favorite words.

And the man was right. Of course he was. Ginny had told her long ago that most addicts had a trigger, something that could kick in and tempt you to revert to destructive patterns long after you thought that behavior had been conquered.

It hadn't been talking about her family that had done it. It had been remembering her uncle and what they'd done together.

No. Not what *they'd* done. What *he'd* done.

What happened is not your fault. It never was. Her therapist's words came through loud and clear.

"Like I said, it's an old habit."

He studied her for several long seconds. "Fair enough. We all have our secrets."

Hardly. She doubted Marcos had a whopper like she did. Sophia had said they'd been raised in an orphanage, but that was hardly something to be ashamed of. Lots of kids grew up under difficult conditions and came out just fine.

Like you did?

Her situation was different. Marcos had probably never felt the urge to gouge himself to the point of drawing blood over being raised in a group home.

Maggie lifted her glass and took a slow, careful

sip. If she didn't ease up on herself, she was going to ruin what had been a pleasant evening. She decided to try to get that easy camaraderie back.

"Who knew these kiosks were open at night?" She crinkled her nose and stared at the now-empty plate, where a tasty seafood paella had been. "Okay, you obviously did or you wouldn't have suggested coming here."

"I come here when I need to get away. Get back to the raw, untamed elements of life. The sound of the waves and the constant shift of the tides seem about as untamed as you can get."

She agreed. And something about the rhythmic crash of the surf was soothing. One type of noise she didn't find jarring and chaotic. She was curious about what else he liked. "What other things do you find raw and untamed?"

"What a deep question for such a beautiful night."

"I'm sorry, I was just—"

"No, don't apologize." He held up a hand. "It's an interesting question. What else do I find raw and untamed?"

He stared back out at the ocean for a moment or two before returning his attention to her. "An eagle soaring high above the earth maybe. A big cat as it takes down its prey." Maggie swallowed hard as his voice got softer, and his eyes trailed over her. "The passion that goes on between a man and a woman."

Holy cow. He didn't believe in beating around the bush, did he? Then again, she'd been the one to ask the question, and if she thought about it, her words had lent themselves to a suggestive answer.

He smiled. "At least I haven't made those nails go back to work. Yet, anyway."

Nails go back to… Oh! She glanced down at her lap where her hand was still and unmoving, fingers relaxed. He was right. Because she felt safe being with him, maybe? Then again, maybe it was the wine.

As if reading her thoughts, he nodded at her empty glass. "Would you like another one?"

She'd only had one. Why not? "Only if you'll join me."

"I can't, Maggie. I have to—how do you say it?—keep my head on straight."

Keep his head on straight.

Or what? He'd let himself fall back into bed with her? Regret it with every fiber of his being the next day? She rubbed her hands on her thighs.

His narrowed eyes were on her again. "What are you thinking? You are so closed—so hidden."

Because she was smarter than she used to be. At

least, she hoped she was. "I was thinking about the wine, that's all."

"My reasons for not wanting another?" His fingers skimmed her forearm. "Because I have to drive us home very soon. That's all."

How did he seem to know exactly what she was thinking? She evidently wasn't as closed as he seemed to think she was. Because he nailed her thoughts more often than not.

And his statement sent a pang of longing through her chest. *I have to drive* us *home...*

She wanted there to be an "us" someday. Oh, not with Marcos, but with someone. She wanted a husband who would love her unconditionally, scars and all. She wanted children she could protect without fail.

His hand was still on her arm, his skin warm against hers, and she shivered.

"You're cold. You should have said something. São Paulo cools off at night, even on the hottest days." He shrugged out of his jacket and stood to drape it over her shoulders.

Her little tremor had nothing to do with being cold, but Maggie wasn't about to tell him that his touch made her insides jiggle like Jell-O. That would just be too embarrassing.

She reached up and tugged his jacket closer, his warm scent surrounding her.

"Would you like to walk along the beach for a few minutes?" He held out a hand.

Without thinking about the consequences, she placed her fingers in his and allowed him to draw her to her feet.

CHAPTER ELEVEN

MARCOS SCOOPED UP her shoes, letting them dangle off his index and middle fingers, while Maggie slid her arms into the sleeves of his tuxedo jacket, holding the edges closed. He struggled not to smile. The thing swallowed her whole, coming down almost to her knees.

Good. Because the last thing he wanted was any of the men on the beach ogling what was…

Not his.

What was wrong with him? She wasn't his. She would never be. They were from two very different worlds.

It had to be the combination of the moonlight and being in a place that he loved. In fact, he'd never brought a woman here before. Maybe for this very reason.

He swallowed as they walked further away from the crowded kiosk and into the dark night, feeling like a huge ball of emotion was trapped just behind his bow-tie—the second time that had happened to him tonight.

Still moving across the sand, he reached up with his free hand and tried to tug the loops on his tie, his fingers getting hung up.

"Here. Let me." Maggie came around to the front, forcing him to stop. She took hold of the tie and deftly unfastened it, her hair gleaming like burnished copper in the moonlight.

"You're good at that."

She shrugged. "My mom taught me. I used to tie these for all the men in our family." Her fingers paused for a second before finishing up, letting the loose ends dangle around his neck.

"Thanks. I hate these things." They reminded him of everything he hadn't had as a child. And re-emphasized all the ways he and Maggie were different. She'd been to enough fancy dinners and events that she knew how to knot a man's tie. Had done it on multiple occasions. Had she done it for anyone outside her immediate family?

Blue eyes came up to meet his. "You look good in one, by the way."

That bubble of emotion made its way back to his throat and his fingers tightened around the straps of her shoes. She thought he looked good?

Marcos started walking again, his dress shoes sinking into the sand—he vaguely wondered if he'd end up ruining them. He tended to do jeans and bare feet when he came here. "I have to wear tuxes periodically to go to fundraisers for the hospital. And now the ballet."

"I'm glad Sophia made it home safely."

"Hmm…" He couldn't help but think that Sophia had somehow orchestrated this whole night—except she really had won the tickets in a game of chance. Maggie had said she'd been with her when her name had been drawn. But she sure hadn't worked very hard to find someone to fill that fourth ticket.

Which was probably a good thing. Because if she'd brought a man as a date for either herself or for Maggie, there might have been trouble. Good thing Sophia hadn't heard about that business card the Carvalho man had handed Maggie.

Speaking of which…

"Did you ever meet up with your fellow American again?"

Maggie frowned. "Who?"

"The plastic surgeon from the conference. The one from your home state."

"Oh, um…" She ducked her head, and Marcos could have sworn her cheeks were tinged with red, although it was hard to tell because the lights from the kiosks were far behind them now. "No. I never called him."

Something about the way she'd said that… "Did he call you?"

"Once or twice. I was always busy at the time."

The tension in his muscles eased, and Marcos allowed the steady sound of the ocean to soothe the wreckage his nerves had become over the course of the evening. If she'd been interested in the guy, she would have either picked up the calls or returned them, neither of which she seemed to have done. Although maybe it was better if he didn't know one way or the other.

He made a decision. He wasn't going to ask about the other doctor again. It was her business. Surely she was smart enough to play it safe.

A gust of sea air blew some loose tendrils of Maggie's hair, and she lifted her face to the wind, giving a soft sigh. "I haven't walked along a beach in ages. So long that I'd forgotten what it's like." She smiled and glanced over at him, her fingers tangling in another strand of hair that sifted across her face. "And I don't think I've ever come to the beach in a long dress."

"You should do it more often. You look beautiful standing here." He didn't know why he'd said the words, they'd come out of their own volition, but they were true. The woman looked stunning, the bottom of her dress tugged by the breeze, the outline of her legs visible beneath his jacket.

Somehow seeing her standing there with his jacket wrapped around her made his chest tighten. He took hold of the lapels and drew her forward, the high heels still dangling from his fingertips.

Her eyes were wide and serious as she peered up at him. "You think I look beautiful?"

"Isn't it obvious?"

She shook her head. "Not to me."

"Then you don't know how to read men very well."

"No. I'm afraid I don't. I never have."

There was such a sad note to her voice that the tightness in his chest turned to a band of steel. "You're pretty good at reading me. Can you guess what I want to do this very second?"

Still gripping the lapels to his coat, he tugged her a few inches closer. "Guess, *querida*."

They were all alone, the night wrapping around them and shielding them from prying eyes.

Her teeth sank into her lip. "Kiss me?"

"Mmm. Yes. Definitely kiss you." He leaned down and slid his lips softly across hers, before retreating. He'd berated himself for crushing her to him behind the trees of the subway station when she'd been timidly exploring him. He was too impatient. Too rough. This time it would be different. "Nice. So very nice."

His lips found hers again, and he applied a little more pressure, his heart pounding out a dangerous rhythm when she responded in kind. Softly. Quietly. But even that had the power to slice right through him.

He kissed along her cheekbone, tasting the slight saltiness of the sea on her skin. "See? You're very good at reading me. Now it's my turn. Should I guess what you want to do?"

"You can try."

He smiled. "Maybe I should rephrase that to say, what I *hope* you want to do."

"And what is that?"

"Kiss me back?"

She glanced down at her toes and several beats went by before she answered. "I'd be lying if I said I didn't want to."

"I'm very glad you're an honest woman, then, Maggie." He released his hold on one side of the jacket and slid his hand into her hair, tilting her head back up. When he lowered his lips this time, he let Maggie take the lead. Let her kiss him however she wanted to.

And it was a heady experience. Her lips nibbled his lower one, slowly kissing her way across his mouth from one side all the way to the other, seeming to take an eternity to finish. The sweetness of it almost overwhelmed him.

The need he'd forced down time and time again over the past month came boiling to the surface, spilling over as he tried to hold himself in check—to keep from grabbing at whatever crumbs she offered him.

"Maggie," he whispered, dragging the back of his knuckles across the hollow beneath her cheek, the velvety texture threatening to unravel him. "I think I want more."

More than kisses. More than petting. He wanted to lay her down in the sand and have her moan beneath him. Just once. He wanted to hear her.

"What do you mean, 'more'?" Her voice was just as soft.

He cupped her face. "Guess."

He was playing a dangerous game. One that could have her bolting at any second. "I—I don't know."

"I think you do." He wasn't sure why he was insisting. Maybe he needed to be certain the wanting went both ways this time—although her body had given up all its secrets as soon as he'd touched her. But he wanted her to openly acknowledge that she felt the same way. That she wanted to be here with *him* and not with the American doctor she'd met.

"You want more than kissing," she whispered.

He nodded.

She moistened her lips. "You want…" She slowly lifted her hand and touched her forefinger to her thumb, making the forbidden sign.

His breath hissed in through his teeth as she stood there.

"You should never flash it at a patient. Or at a man. Unless you want something bad to happen to you."

Had she remembered those words? Remembered what had happened afterwards?

He took hold of her hand, and brought it to his mouth, his eyes holding hers as he kissed the circle she'd formed with her fingers. "Yes. That's what I want. I want it very badly. But only if you do, too."

"I do."

He didn't want to offer her an escape, but he knew his conscience wouldn't let him take the easy way out. Not this time. "I want there to be no misunderstandings, Maggie. I want you. Right now, with the waves pounding behind us. The night all around us." He undid her fingers and twined his through hers. "Say that's what you want, too."

"It's what I want." There was no hesitation as she said the words.

He kissed her again. Firmer this time, letting her feel some of what was coursing through him. She twined her arms around his neck in answer, and she must have gone up on tiptoe because suddenly she was higher, closer to his mouth, closer to the center of his desire.

Marcos forgot about everything other than the feel of this woman against him. Her scent. His hands going beneath the jacket to the bare skin of her back.

He planned to enjoy this night. To make it last. To take her home afterwards and make love to her again in his bed. To wake up with her beside him.

Deep inside, a flicker of fear came to life as he wondered if one night would be enough. Or if he'd be left wanting much, much more.

More than she was willing to give.

Or, worse, more than he was willing to receive.

He drew her backwards, drugging her with a chaotic blend of kisses until she found herself near a lifeguard shack—unmanned at this time of night.

She vaguely wondered how often this scene had been played out in Marcos's past. How many times he'd made love to someone on this very beach.

The thought didn't last long because as soon as her back pressed against the wooden wall of the structure he was kissing her again, sliding both hands into her hair and muttering his disapproval at her tight chignon. Lips still against hers, he murmured, "Why do women torture us with these hairstyles? Turn around."

He took hold of her shoulders and turned her toward the building, where a tiny window gave a dim reflection of her flushed features. He pulled out one hairpin, allowing a winding lock of hair to fall free, which he twirled around his finger. "Much better, yes?"

Leaning forward, he pressed his cheek against hers, chin nudging aside his jacket to rest on her bare shoulder, the prickles of stubble sending shivers through her. "I could stare at you all night." He laid a kiss on the side of her neck. "And I will."

Another shudder gripped her as a wave of raw desire went over her. He planned to keep her here the entire night?

Yes. She wanted that…wanted this man with a desperation that was unmatched by anything she'd felt before.

He lifted his head and plucked more pins from her hair, letting strand after strand fall in soft waves around her shoulders.

"Can anyone see us?"

He smiled. "No. This is a long way from the nearest kiosk." Pulling the very last hairpin, he slid them all into the pocket of his tuxedo trousers then reached up to comb his fingers through the locks. "That's better. I wish you could see yourself, *querida*. You look as wild and untamed as the sea."

The last thing she was interested in was looking at herself, not when he was standing just behind her like some dark Adonis. Not when the back of his hand was trailing across her cheekbone, down the side of her neck, along her shoulder, the jacket almost falling free.

"Marcos." Her voice was breathless. "You're driving me crazy."

"I want you crazy." His fingertips whispered down her arms until he reached her hands, threading his fingers through the backs of hers. Lifting them, he placed her palms on the warm wood in front of her, holding them there as his body crowded hers from behind. She felt the hard ridge of flesh against the base of her spine, even through his suit coat.

She didn't get a chance to enjoy it, though, because Marcos spun her back into his arms as gracefully as if they were dancing. He then scooped her into his arms and carried her through the open doorway of the shack, kicking it closed behind them.

"Just in case," he whispered. "I want you all to myself."

Oh, Lord. This was actually going to happen. She was in Marcos's arms, and he wanted her.

He went to his knees, before lowering her gently onto the wooden planks, his jacket cushioning her back. He followed her down, his lips covering hers in a flurry of light kisses that had her arching up for more, all thoughts of their location lost in the rush of sensation.

She bit back a gasp as he leaned up and peeled the top of her dress down, revealing a lack of hardware beneath it. The cool night air brushed across her nipples, bringing them to stiff peaks.

"*Meu Deus.* I was afraid of this. I've wondered all night long what you could possibly have on under this dress." He gave her a pained smile. "Thank God I didn't know until now."

He hadn't bothered taking off the tuxedo jacket, so she lay with the coat spread open, her dress pulled down and her breasts on full display. It seemed obscene somehow, and incredibly erotic. Especially when he leaned down and licked the very tip of one of them, sending a shaft of ecstasy shooting through her. Suddenly she just wanted him to hike up her dress and be done with it. Who needed to get undressed anyway?

As he continued to lap across her nipple with wet strokes of his tongue, her eyes fluttered shut and she pressed closer, unable to stop herself. He rewarded her by closing his mouth around her and sucking hard. Gritting her teeth, she struggled not to moan, the sound going through the inside of her head instead.

Just when she thought he was going to drive her insane, he sat up, pulling her up with him. "Let's get these clothes off, shall we?"

Yes. Please.

Suddenly, their location didn't matter. All she wanted was to be as close to him as humanly possible.

He tugged off the jacket, one arm at a time, before folding it into a makeshift pallet on the floor. Drawing a line across the top edge of the dress where it lay beneath her breasts, he followed it around to the back. "And this little beauty, does it have a *zipper*?"

The word, the same in English and Brazilian

Portuguese, slid from his mouth with that peculiar accent she found so damned hot.

"No. It has hooks on the straps."

"Ah, I've found them." Wrapping his arms around her, he held the dress with one hand, while the other undid the fasteners on either side. When he let go, the fabric fell around her hips. She watched his Adam's apple dip beneath his shirt collar then come back up. "You're so incredibly lovely. I'm glad the moon is out tonight."

The ends of his bow-tie still dangled around his neck, and Maggie chanced tugging it free of his collar. She let it drop to the floor beside her.

Marcos unbuttoned his shirt and then stood to pull it loose from his trousers.

Oh, Lord. She was right on a level with his…

And what he wanted was so very obvious.

It was what she wanted, too.

She pulled in a careful breath then started to shimmy out of the rest of her clothes, only to have Marcos stop her. "I want to do that. I've been dreaming of easing that dress over your body all night long. I couldn't even concentrate on the ballet."

So she sat there as he slowly slid his elegant black belt from his trousers one loop at a time, then rolled it around his hand a time or two in a way that made her eyes widen. He gave her a wicked grin. "Worried I'll use this? Or are you hoping, *querida*?"

Use it how?

He waited a beat or two. "All you have to do is say the word, Maggie. I can make it happen."

Was that what she wanted?

Yes! No!

She had no idea what this man was going to do next. Or how far he would go. Suddenly, she wanted it all. Everything he had to give. But she couldn't get the words out of her throat.

He lifted a brow then coiled the belt the rest of the way and set it on the windowsill beside him. Still in plain view. Her mouth went dry.

"Next time, maybe," he murmured.

Next time.

The man wound her up in a way that went beyond comprehension. Just with a word. A touch of his hand.

But right now all she really wanted him to do was hurry.

As if he read her mind, he unfastened his pants then unzipped them.

When he knelt again and reached for the bottom of her dress, she started to lift her hips to help him take it off, but he tunneled up underneath it instead, his hands gliding up her bare thighs until he found her panties. He made a sound as he hooked his fingers around the upper elastic. "I wondered about this as well. You're willing to go bare on top, but not on bottom. So many secrets to unravel. But you won't be needing these." As soon as he said it, he yanked her underwear down her legs and tossed them to the side.

His hands went back to her dress, but instead of pushing it up or taking it off, he lifted the green fabric away from her thighs, like a surgical drape and then ducked beneath it. Too late, she realized what he was going to do, and she reflexively tried to close her legs, but she couldn't, because he was braced on his arms, holding them apart.

Oh, Lord.

Anticipation gripped her, and suddenly she was trapped in a swift-moving current of desire she was powerless to fight. She struggled to find something to hang onto, but all she could do was hold perfectly still and wait.

The heat of his breath was the first thing she felt as it washed across her most sensitive area. Her eyes closed, stomach muscles clenching and un-clenching as his hands wrapped around her upper thighs, thumbs strumming across the flesh a time or two before he pushed them wider.

He said something, the words low and unfamiliar, but his tone made her think he was invoking some higher power. Maybe she needed to do the same.

Do it! Oh, please, do it.

The litany went through her brain, repeating again and again, until she thought she would scream.

When that first touch came, his tongue was as soft as the words he'd just whispered, but it didn't matter. Her reaction was immediate. She was so ready, wanted him so badly that she went off like a shot, the air sawing in and out of her lungs as she silently bucked beneath him, struggling to process the torrent of sensations pouring through her. Not even that little device she'd bought at one of the naughtier shops had prepared her for the force of being back under Marcos's spell, having him touch her again.

When he finally came out from beneath her dress, he sat back on his heels for a second or two. "You take my breath away."

He wasn't the only one. She could barely breathe. And, crazily, she still wanted him just as badly as she had a second ago.

His hands went to her dress and tugged it over

her hips and laid it beside her. Out came his wallet, the little packet inside.

And then he was free of his clothing, nudging her thighs back apart and covering her body with his—flesh to flesh, this time.

This was right. So very right.

"*Deus*, I want you. Want…this." His hips jerked forward, pushing into her with a single thrust that knocked the wind from her lungs a second time. For a moment she lay still, trying to absorb it all, then her arms went around him as she drew him closer. Letting him fill her.

He started to move. Too slowly.

She didn't want slow—had waited far too long for this. She wanted deep. Hard. Fast.

Heart pounding and blood rushing through her ears, she used her hips to tell him what she wanted. He responded instantly, his body and hands urging hers to fly again—muttering gritty, nonsensical things in Portuguese, the sounds amplified tenfold as he pressed his lips against her ear. Instead of grating on her nerves, the whispers made her feel cherished, as he told her exactly how being with her made him feel. With every thrust the words grew more heated, his groans rougher. Half of the sounds meant nothing to her, the other half…

Marcos used the other half to rush her toward

the edge of a steep cliff and then didn't hesitate to shove her over the side, gripping her hands as he followed her, flying into space and falling...falling, the ground rising up to meet her at a frightening rate.

Shattered, she lay there, eyes closed as his weight settled on top of her, his gusting breath taking the place of his groans. Then she was moving. Onto her side, his hand on her hip as he steadied her on his jacket, before sliding into her hair. His lips pressed against her forehead, feathering back down to her ear.

"Tu és perfeita. Magía."

She wasn't magic. Neither was she perfect. Not by a long shot. But it was nice to hear him say it.

Smiling, she tried to gather her thoughts into something coherent. But they had been flung far and wide, never settling into place. Just like a shell tossed about by the waves.

Marcos leaned up on one elbow on the rough boards, his palm skimming over the curves of her side before cupping her hip.

He'd said she was perfect. *He* was the one who was perfect.

Thick stubble lined his jaw, even though he'd been clean-shaven at the beginning of the evening.

His dark eyes roved over her as if he couldn't get enough.

She could lie here for ever.

Then he found the first of her scars.

His fingertips slid down her outer thigh, pausing as if noticing the difference in texture there. His eyes followed, narrowing in the dim light as he leaned up a little further. Before she could reach for her dress and yank it over the marks, a low curse broke the silence between them.

Then he was back. His gaze glued to hers.

"What are these?"

CHAPTER TWELVE

THOSE SCARS WERE more than skin-deep, but Maggie had refused to talk about them last night, saying they were in her past.

But the way she'd dug her nails into her skin back at the kiosk—her so-called bad habit—made him think the two were related. That the marks were self-inflicted. The way she'd slapped his hand away and tried to hide them with her own had set alarm bells off in his skull. But there were too many of them, her hand couldn't even begin to cover them.

They weren't just in her past.

Because he'd seen her. At the conference. At the beach.

And when she'd grabbed her panties and tugged them up her legs, he'd seen scars marring her other thigh as well, cementing his theory. Either she'd hurt herself or someone else had done it to her.

He was supposed to be at the conference with her right now, but he'd left a note with her doorman, begging off, saying he needed to check in on Stácia, which he did. But the reality was he didn't want to face her. Not only because of what had happened between them last night but because he wasn't sure what to say to her.

He'd stood there staring at her in that little shack as she'd hauled her dress up and over her hips, breasts—holding it in place when he'd made no move to help her fasten it in back.

The thought of taking her back to his place and making love to her for the rest of the night had imploded right in front of him. He'd dressed in silence, sliding his belt back through the loops of his slacks and wondering what she'd been thinking as he'd stood there and teased her with it earlier. No wonder she hadn't responded to his words. The joke suddenly tasted sour on his tongue.

Had someone actually hurt her? Burned her? Or had she done it all herself?

The questions had gone round and round in his skull as Maggie had sat stiff and unyielding in the passenger seat on the ride back to her apartment And now she was at the conference. Alone.

And if Dr. Carvalho is there as well?

He pressed his thumb and forefinger to the bridge of his nose. That wasn't something he could control. In fact, there wasn't much he *could* control right now.

Except his job. Which was what he should be doing. He picked up the first patient's folder from his desk and flipped it open, then reached for a pen.

A quick knock came at the door, and Sophia popped her head in with a smile. "Hey, are you busy?"

Great. Just what he needed. A question-and-answer session with the world's nosiest nurse.

"I'm about to be. What do you need?" He allowed a portion of his frustration to show through in his voice before regretting it and softening his words. "How's your headache this morning, by the way?"

"I've been taking ibuprofen for it. I think my allergies are acting up." She stepped inside and shut the door behind her. "Sorry for leaving you in the lurch last night. I know you really didn't want to go to the ballet in the first place. You went because I pushed you into going."

He leaned back. Interesting. He'd assumed Sophia's enthusiasm for life had just gotten the better of her. He was getting a hint that this had been more than that. "So why did you?"

"Because you've turned into a stuffy old man."

Old man.

The term Maggie had quoted her as saying last night.

Marcos's brows went up. "I hardly think thirty-five qualifies as elderly in today's society."

"You know what I mean."

She dropped into the chair across from him, and he sighed. This didn't bode well for a quick exit on her part. "You never go out and have fun," she said.

"You know this for a fact, do you?" He had plenty of fun. Besides, he loved his job. Maybe that was the only diversion he needed. The nightlife had never really appealed to Marcos—the discos, the bars, the excesses of Carnival.

He was fine spending a quiet night on the beach. Alone.

At least, he had been fine with that, until last night. The result of that lapse was exactly the reason he didn't take women out there. Making an exception to that particular rule had just complicated his life—and his job—as there was no getting around working with Maggie for the next four months. Unless he turned her over to another doctor. Which he wouldn't do. Maggie was a good neurosurgeon. She deserved to do what she'd come here to do. Serve out her internship under him.

And that did not include her being *under* him in the baser sense.

He shifted in his chair, trying not to wonder about the ethics of what had happened between them on the beach. It wasn't as if she were a twenty-one-year-old virgin he'd seduced.

And it definitely hadn't been him who'd flashed that hand signal last night.

Sophia picked up a paperclip from his desk and fiddled with it. "I worry about you. I always have."

He couldn't hold back a smile. Yes, she had. Even though she'd been a few years younger than him, she'd taken him under her wing at the orphanage, pulling him by the hand from place to place to show him where the cafeteria was, where the place to pick up his clothes was, where the best spots to be alone were. Marcos had always imagined himself Sophia's self-appointed guardian, but maybe it had been the other way around.

"I know you worry, but I'm a big boy now."

She crinkled her nose with an answering smile. "And I'm a big girl. But that didn't stop you from calling me this morning and chewing me out for taking the subway by myself. I texted Maggie every step of the way."

"If you'd let me know you weren't feeling well, we could have all left together." Only then he wouldn't have gotten to spend the rest of the evening in Maggie's company. And despite how it had ended, it had been one of the most incredible nights of his life.

Because she's a foreigner. She's exotic. Mysterious.

He swallowed hard. *Magic.*

Hell, he had to stop thinking of her like that. There was nothing magic about animal lust between two human beings. Nothing magic about those scars riddling her pale flesh.

They'd had sex, and now it was over. They'd go about their business just like every other member of the animal kingdom.

It was more than that, and you know it.

"I didn't want you to go home just because of me," Sophia said. "I wanted you to enjoy yourself."

She dropped the paperclip back on his desk, and the click as it landed echoed through the room. "How was the rest of the ballet?"

How did he tell her that he and Maggie hadn't stayed for the rest of the performance? They'd left almost as soon as Sophia had. "I don't know much about that kind of thing. I guess it was okay."

There, not exactly a lie. More like an evasion. He glanced at his watch, hoping to call a halt to this interview pretty soon. "Are you off duty?"

"Nope, just on a break. I wanted to stop in and check on…" Her hand suddenly went to the back of her head, and she leaned forward for a second or two before straightening back up in her seat.

"Sophia? What's wrong?"

She started to shake her head, then gasped. "Nothing, my head just feels a little…" Sitting very still, she pulled in air with slow, careful breaths.

Marcos came around the desk. "Is your headache worse?"

"I don't know what's wrong. I took some medicine for it. The pills don't normally wear off this quickly." She got up suddenly, her face turning pasty white. "Oh, I think I'm going to be…"

She rushed over to the trashcan beside his desk and dropped to her knees. She vomited. Then again.

Marcos knelt beside her as she clutched the sides of the plastic container and retched over and over. He held her shoulders to steady her. "Hell, you're burning up, Soph. I want to get some bloodwork. And maybe a spinal tap."

"No. It's probably just a migraine."

"You said it was allergies a minute ago."

"I thought it…" The sentence died as her stomach heaved again, but there was nothing left to come up this time. She moaned, her hands covering her face as she breathed in and out as if trying to get her body back under control.

"Where does it hurt, exactly?"

She didn't try to answer him, just laid a hand across the back of her neck where it connected with her skull.

"Don't move." He went around to his desk and hit the button to his secretary. "I need a wheelchair in here. And clear my calendar. Also, I need you to page Dr. Pfeiffer and get her out of that convention and back to the hospital as soon as possible. Tell her it's urgent."

"Yes, sir."

He went back to Sophia, ruing that he'd ever doubted her story last night. She'd finally let go of the wastebin but it was obvious something was very wrong.

"I'm sorry about that, Marcos."

Brushing off her apology, he went down on his haunches beside her. "That's the least of my worries right now. Was your headache this bad at the ballet?"

"No, it was just nagging. It was a little worse

when I woke up, but the medicine did help, or I wouldn't have come to work this morning."

"Of course not." His door opened, and an orderly appeared with a wheelchair. He stood then lifted Sophia and placed her gently in it. "We're going to get you into a room and draw some blood."

"I feel so silly. It's probably nothing."

"Probably. But we're going to make sure." From the way his insides were knotting and releasing, he wasn't as sure as she was. And Maggie was probably a half-hour out, even if she got the message and left the conference immediately. Thank God he'd needed some breathing space this morning and had sent her on without him. Or he wouldn't have been here for Sophia.

Following the wheelchair from his office to the bank of elevators, he punched the floor into the main keypad and waited as it flashed the letter of the next available elevator. The orderly pushed her over to it just as it pinged its arrival. Once in it, Marcos took her hand as she leaned her head against the back of the wheelchair, eyes closed. Every once in a while he could see her wince as a wave of pain went through her.

Hell, he hoped it wasn't a brain bleed. "Still hurt?"

"Shh. I'm concentrating on not throwing up right now."

He set a hand on her shoulder and gave a soft squeeze. "Don't worry about anything, *querida*. We're going to figure this out."

This time Sophia didn't argue or say that he was overreacting. From the temperature of her skin through her blouse, her fever had to be approaching thirty-nine degrees, high under any circumstances. But it helped put the brain-bleed theory to rest. There was an infection of some sort in her body. Meningitis, maybe, like he'd originally suspected. Or it could even be a cerebral abscess. "Have you had a sinus infection or dental problems recently, Soph?"

Her eyes fluttered open, and she fixed him with a glare. Okay, she wasn't going to be a good patient. Not many healthcare workers were. "Allergies, remember? My sinuses have been backed up for weeks."

The pollution in São Paulo tended to aggravate allergies and make them worse on days when the haze hung low over the city. If her sinuses really had been full for a while, an infection could have settled in, which in turn could have traveled to her brain and formed a pocket. Not a common occurrence, and definitely not good.

The elevator opened on the third floor, and Marcos walked ahead, motioning for the orderly to follow him. He checked in at the nurses' station and glanced at the chart, noting there was an empty room just around the corner.

The nurse did a double take when she saw who was in the chair. "Sophia, what happened?"

Sophia waved off her colleague's concern and closed her eyes once again. Her bubbly personality had suddenly gone dark, which was another sign that things were not as they should be.

They got her settled into the room, and Marcos handed her an emesis basin, smiling faintly when she sent him another weak glare, but she took it. One of the other nurses came in, and Marcos gave her a list of instructions. Once she'd had her blood drawn, he wanted a sample of her spinal fluid. "We're going to do some poking and prodding. You know the routine."

"I hate needles."

He blinked. "You're a nurse, for God's sake."

"Exactly. I'm the one who does the jabbing." Her hand went to her head again, despite the playful words.

At least she could joke. He'd thought for a minute or two she might go down in his office. And the thought of the world without Sophia if she'd caught something really serious…

No, he'd already lost too many people: his father and mother…and Lucas. He wasn't about to lose Sophia as well.

"Maybe I have dengue."

Marcos shook his head. "I haven't heard of any cases in the last month or so. Let's just do some tests and see what we've got."

Leaving the room as the nurse prepared to draw blood, he spied Maggie coming down the hall, her heels clicking on the linoleum floor as she hurried to the nurses' station, beige skirt snug around her hips. That was fast. She still had the lanyard from the conference around her neck.

"Maggie."

Whirling around, she stared at him for a second before squaring her shoulders and walking toward him. Good, she was going to face him head on, rather than try to avoid him.

"The message said something was wrong with Sophia. What happened?"

"She collapsed in my office. Severe headache, vomiting, fever."

"Oh, no." Her eyes focused somewhere below his chin. "Meningitis? Encephalitis?"

He could almost see the wheels working in her

head. "If it's meningitis, it would be viral as she's been vaccinated against the bacterial version, just like the rest of our staff."

"Could it be something tropical? It has to be infectious."

"Unless it's two separate agents at work." He glanced back at the door of the room. "I'm taking her to the imaging department, just in case."

Maggie frowned. "You need to call someone else in on the case. You know that, right?"

"Yes. That's why you're here."

Her brows went up. "What?"

"I want you to take her case. You're not related to her."

"Sophia and I are friends. We went shopping together. I shouldn't be treating her any more than you should. If something is going on with her brain, you need to call in another neurologist, someone impartial. Surely you could ask a colleague you trust to take this on."

"I thought I was, actually." His mouth tightened, even though he knew he wasn't being fair. In reality, he'd hoped to keep the letter of the law by having Maggie listed as her attending, while still calling all the shots himself.

Her fingers went to his arm. "Marcos, I would

if I could, but I care about her too much to trust my own judgment."

"Fine. I'll call Dr. Romildo."

She didn't back down, like he'd hoped she might. Instead, she said, "You're doing the right thing."

He hoped so. Because he sure hadn't been making the best decisions lately—not about letting the night go by without checking on Sophia. And not about taking Maggie to the beach.

But from here on out he was going to be smart. Just like he'd promised his father he'd be.

CHAPTER THIRTEEN

"THANK GOD."

Maggie sank into the chair across from Marcos's desk when the results came back in. Viral meningitis, just as he'd predicted. Seven to ten days' recuperation time and Sophia should be as good as new.

"They're going to discharge her today, but I'm taking her home with me. Which means you'll have to go to the conference without me for a couple of days."

The thought should have dismayed her, but it didn't. It had actually been a relief not to have to face him this morning after what they'd done. And the thought of extending that reprieve was an even bigger relief. Their interactions had been a train wreck from almost day one. And she didn't seem to have the will to say no.

And to flash that sign at him at a public beach? What kind of craziness was that?

The kind of craziness that had her hormones

jumping like mad when he'd slowly brought her hand to his mouth and kissed her fingers.

Lord. And here she was thinking about it all over again. She sat up straight, curling her fingers in her lap and twining them together in a knot.

"That's fine. I've understood the seminars for the most part. There are a couple other ones I'd like to attend tomorrow. Do you need me at the hospital for anything?"

"No. You go and enjoy." He rubbed the back of his neck. "Which seminars are they?"

"I'll have to look at the program, but I thought I'd go to the 'Innovations in Cranioplasty' one, especially after observing Stácia's surgery."

"Cranioplasty? Is that part of the neurology track?"

"I think it's listed as a dual-track seminar. Neurology and plastic surgery, as it deals with cosmetic elements of skull reconstruction as well as the functional ones."

One brow went up. "Maybe you'll run into the plastic surgeon from New Jersey there."

Maggie couldn't tell whether he was hoping to deflect her attention away from himself or if he was just making idle conversation. Either way, the offhand remark stuck in her craw. "Maybe I will. That would be lucky, wouldn't it?"

"If you do, make sure you pick up a business card for me. I might just have to look him up."

She went from irritation to shock in the space of a nanosecond. Was that a veiled threat? No. Of course not. He just meant because the man was Brazilian by birth, that's all. Maybe he wanted to discuss treatment differences between the States and Brazil.

Unsure if he expected her to answer him, she decided to prevaricate. "I'll do that. I'll let him know you're interested in speaking with him."

He gave her a slow smile. "Or I could just make a copy of the card he gave you instead."

A second wave of panic went through her when she thought he actually meant to call the surgeon and say something about last night. She immediately squashed that idea. Why on earth would he do that? It wasn't like last night had been special in any way. To either of them.

But just in case… "Sorry. I left it by the phone at my apartment."

The coolness in his eyes dropped another twenty degrees. Great. The last thing she wanted to do was start a war with the doctor she was supposed to be working with—or to make things more awkward than they already were.

Dumb move, Maggie.

She didn't want Marcos thinking she played the field, jumping from one bed to another. Although surely he could tell by her behavior that she wasn't the most experienced woman on the planet when it came to intimate relations. And she could have died when he'd asked her about those marks on her legs, his fingers tracking over them one by one.

Suppressing a shiver at the memory, she stood. "I want to go up and check on Sophia, and then I think I'll go home. It was a long night last…"

Her voice trailed away when she realized exactly why she felt so tired and sluggish today. And exactly where she'd spent a good part of her evening.

"Yes, Maggie. It was a long night." He stood and placed his hands flat on his desk, leaning forward slightly as he looked her in the eye. "I expect you to remember each and every minute of it as you attend those seminars."

Shifting in her chair for the fifth time, Maggie closed her eyes and cursed Marcos Pinheiro for what he'd done to her. Dr. Carvalho had waved at her from across the conference room before getting up and moving to the chair next to hers. "Hi. I wondered if I'd see you again before the conference was over."

She'd given him a half-hearted greeting and slid

a little lower in her chair. Of course the cranio-plasty lecture would be the last seminar of the day. And of course Marcos had said she might see the other doctor there.

If Marcos had been here with her, this probably wouldn't have happened because he'd be occupying the chair the plastic surgeon was in. And she was also more than a little irritated at her boss for that last loaded statement he'd lobbed at her before she'd left his office.

"I expect you to remember each and every minute of it as you attend those seminars."

She did. She remembered it all. And those memories were doing awful things to her equilibrium.

Luckily, by the time she'd arrived the lecture had been getting under way, so there hadn't been a lot of time for chit-chat before the speaker had got up to the podium, but now that it was almost over? Was she going to have to stand around and talk to her fellow American—or, worse, turn down that offer of drinks he'd made last week?

After what had happened with Marcos, she didn't see herself wanting any more casual outings with men. She obviously was not to be trusted to keep things at a superficial level.

Only when it came to Marcos. Maybe her sub-conscious was right. Because there was no heart-flipping or quivery feelings low in her belly from Dr. Carvalho's proximity. But he also wasn't leaning into her and forcing himself into her personal space. He was being a perfect gentleman. He seemed genuinely happy to talk to someone who spoke English.

She turned her head during a lull at the end of the seminar as the lecturer paused so audience members could jot down information from several of the slides he'd presented earlier. "Didn't any other doctors from your hospital come to the conference?"

He glanced back at her with a friendly smile. "No one else at our practice understands Portuguese. I told them I'd take notes and let them know if I learned anything interesting."

"And have you? Learned anything interesting?" She found herself smiling back, unable to resist his easy charm. There was nothing threatening about his demeanor in the least. Marcos had been wrong about him.

"I have, actually."

"Really? What?" She relaxed into her chair, leaning her chin on the palm of her hand as she looked at him. She was actually grateful to have something to take her mind off the turmoil of the past week.

"For one thing, I learned that staring daggers at someone is not just an expression."

Her chin slipped off her hand. "I'm sorry?"

He inclined his head toward the far wall without actually looking in that direction. "Isn't that the doctor you were with when we met the first time? He looked at me exactly the same way when I handed you my card."

Oh, God. Her glance skated toward the other side of the room and she spotted Marcos, who was leaning against the wall, his strong arms crossed over his chest.

And, yes. Those were daggers. Aimed not at the man beside her but at her.

"Um. Yes, I'm actually doing an internship under him at the hospital. I hope nothing's wrong."

He gave a soft laugh. "Oh, I think something is wrong all right. If you could assure him I only have the purest of motives, I'd appreciate it. I'm not looking to go home and asking one of my colleagues to put my nose back in its correct location."

"Oh, I'm sure he's just…" What could she say, really? She and Marcos weren't a couple, and they never would be.

They'd had a one-night stand. Okay, two, if you counted that day in his car. But she had no intention of hanging around Brazil and starting something with a man she found dangerous on so many levels. "We have a friend who contracted meningitis. I'm sure he's just here to give me an update on her condition."

"I'm sure that must be what it is." His dubious look said he wasn't buying her explanation.

Well, neither was she. But there was no way she was going to cringe down in her chair and let Marcos make her nervous.

Instead, she gave the other doctor a brilliant smile, the brightest one she could dredge up, even though a strange sense of excitement and foreboding was beginning to pump through her veins. "Don't worry. He's harmless."

Really? Really, Maggie? That's not what you thought to yourself a few minutes ago.

The screen went dark and the lecturer thanked everyone for their attention, moving away so the conference co-ordinator could get up and give instruction about the next day's events.

"I have to tell you, he looks like a regular bastard to me."

She couldn't hold back a laugh. "Do you think so? He's not as bad as all that."

Although she had to admit he did look like one, glowering at her from across the room like he was.

"Seriously. You aren't letting him bully you, are you?" He glanced back at Marcos, a challenging glare marring his rugged face this time. "I could hang around for a while if you want me to."

She drew in a deep breath, her laughter drying up. "No, I'll be fine. I'd let you know if there was a problem."

Maggie realized she was telling the truth. Gone were the days when she'd silently accept someone forcing her to do something she didn't want without the slightest murmur of protest.

Dr. Carvalho touched her arm then stood. "If you're sure, I'm going to slide out, then. My email address and phone number are on the back of that card I gave you. Get in touch with me when you get back to the States, okay?"

"I will." Suddenly she knew she would contact him. There was something about the other doctor that struck her as vaguely familiar, though she wasn't sure why. Maybe it was because he was nothing like Marcos, whose hard, haughty attitude kept everyone at a distance.

Didn't she have barriers that did the same?

Probably. But knowing that didn't magically make them disappear. But maybe she could work on it. Start trusting men again, little by little. Maybe even beginning with Dr. Carvalho.

And Marcos?

Possibly. If he'd let her.

She watched as the plastic surgeon made his way between the chairs to the exit on the opposite side of the room from where Marcos was perched. She guessed he didn't want a confrontation if none was needed.

A whisper of air drew her attention to the fact that she was still seated, and someone had just dropped into the chair next to hers.

She swallowed then willed herself to turn and face the inevitable. Marcos crossed a foot over his knee and studied her for a moment. Dressed in a black button-down shirt and equally dark dress slacks, he looked as elegant in business clothes as he had in that tuxedo.

"Enjoying yourself?" he murmured.

"As a matter of fact, I am." Her chin popped just a bit higher as she dared him to say anything about the other doctor's presence.

"I thought you might like an update on Sophia's condition." He glanced around the emptying room. "And I wanted to offer you a ride back to the hospital—unless you're planning to take the subway."

At rush hour? She wasn't interested in doing that again. She'd planned to catch a cab instead. "Oh. You didn't have to do that."

His eyes softened a fraction. "I know. I wanted to. And I did want to let you know that Sophia is better, in case you went straight back to your apartment, rather than stopping by the hospital."

"Has she been released?"

"Yes. She's at my house."

"Good, I'm glad she won't be alone."

His lips curved slightly. "Sophia tends to worry about other people being alone, rather than her. She always has."

Something about the way he said it made her chest ache. Was he talking about himself as a boy at the orphanage…something he'd still not mentioned?

She decided to steer clear of that subject. "Thank you for coming to tell me in person. It was thoughtful."

"Thoughtful." He seemed to mull over that word. "I wouldn't exactly call it that."

Had he really been worried she might hook up with the plastic surgeon? If so, he must have been surprised when he'd found her sitting beside the man. "Just so you know. He sat with me, rather than the other way around. And he was a perfect gentleman. He wants to keep in touch after he gets back to the States."

The stiff set of Marcos's shoulders seemed to soften further. "He's going back soon, then."

"I don't know. He didn't say, but I imagine so. There are only a couple more days left of the conference, and I don't think I'll see him again."

"So, will you? Keep in touch with him?"

No reason not to be honest. "Yes, I think so. We're from the same state. He probably comes home to visit from time to time."

"I see."

Maggie's emotions were all tangled up inside her right now. She didn't know how Marcos could see, when she herself couldn't make heads or tails of anything.

She only knew that her stomach had that quivery sensation she'd been missing while Dr. Carvalho had sat beside her.

And her fingers were tingling with the old familiar pins and needles that had plagued her on and off for the past month. Why?

She stared down at them, trying to figure out what was happening to her.

Marcos wasn't a threat to her so she didn't understand what was causing it, or why she...

The realization came to her in a flash, and the blood drained from her head, making her feel dizzy.

She knew why her fingers were tingling and what the warning sensation meant.

Marcos had the power to hurt her—really hurt her—if she wasn't careful. Not physically, like her uncle had done. But emotionally. Not because of anything he did but because of her own stupidity in not protecting herself.

If she fell for this man, Maggie knew beyond a shadow of a doubt it would not end well for her. And she knew that was not a chance she wanted to take.

So from here on out she was going to have to be very, very careful and keep her distance. Just like Marcos did on a daily basis.

Maybe the best way to do that was to tell him about her past. It had seemed to destroy what she'd had with her ex-boyfriend, even though she'd kept some parts to herself. Why would it be any different with Marcos? As soon as he knew the truth about her, about what she'd done to herself, he'd go running for the hills.

When to do it, that was the question.

How about on the ride to the hospital?

Yes. The sooner the better.

Now all she had to do was actually work up the courage to pull the switch and put an end to things once and for all.

CHAPTER FOURTEEN

MAGGIE WAS QUIET as they got into his car to ride back to the hospital.

Why wouldn't she be? You glared at her from across the room like a jealous lover for a good fifteen minutes before either of them noticed you were there.

She was probably furious.

He was pretty damned angry with himself, for that matter. The other doctor hadn't tried anything. Hadn't slid his arm around the back of her chair, or even touched her, other than that one quick finger-to-the-forearm gesture as he'd said goodbye.

But ever since Maggie had walked out his office yesterday, he'd been eaten up by some type of tension he could only attribute to jealousy. All because she'd said she was going to the cranioplasty seminar.

His attitude infuriated him. He had no hold

over Maggie. No right to ask or expect anything from her.

And he'd never promised her a thing.

She was here for a few more months and that was it. Dr. Carvalho was from her home state. Of course they'd keep in touch.

And he himself? Would he keep in touch with her once she was gone?

He swallowed down the wash of stomach acid that bubbled up his esophagus. There'd be no reason to contact her ever again.

And he knew he wanted to. He wished he could casually suggest they get drinks or say, "Hey, let's stay in touch once you get back to the States."

But he knew he wouldn't. He'd never been the type of person who formed strong attachments.

A hopeful part of his subconscious perked up. *What about Sophia?*

That wasn't the same thing at all. Sophia had attached herself to him, not the other way around. He'd formed no lasting relationships since his brother had been adopted by another family.

Maybe it's time you changed that.

With a girl who was only here for a short period of time?

No, thanks. He wasn't into that kind of masochism.

His lips curved up. No, he was into the kind that provided the most powerful physical rush of pleasure he'd ever experienced, while supplying him with enough mental torture to last quite a few years.

"What's so funny?"

He glanced to the side to see Maggie frowning at him in much the same way as he'd frowned at her in that lecture hall. "Nothing much. Just thinking of joining the BDSM movement."

Maggie's eyes widened. "I'm sorry?"

"Nothing. Bad attempt at a joke."

One that was totally on him.

His thumb rubbed along the steering-wheel as he braked for a red light. "So how was the conference?"

"Fine. How was your day at the hospital?"

"Pretty typical. No surgeries, though, which was good. We did have a teenager come in with a severe concussion."

"What happened? Car accident?"

"Yes. She should be fine, though. No lasting effects."

"No lasting effects." The words were soft. Sad.

He turned and glanced at her. "Maggie, are you okay?"

She licked her lips. "Can we stop somewhere for a minute?"

An alarm went off somewhere in his head, similar to the one he'd heard when Sophia had almost collapsed in his office, although Maggie seemed perfectly composed. Too composed, if anything. Almost plastic.

"Sure. Just let me find a spot."

He pulled off the highway and found the only spot he could, in the no-parking zone near the city park. They wouldn't be here long enough for it to matter.

Turning the car off, he shifted to face her. "What's going on?"

Maggie sucked down a long, deep breath then released it on a sigh. "You asked me about those marks on my legs."

He nodded, his stomach tightening. After all that coaxing and demanding, why had she suddenly decided to tell him now?

Lifting her hands so that the backs of them faced him, she wiggled her fingertips. "I made them with these."

He'd been right. Despite his suspicions, a thread of nausea wound through his stomach at the matter-of-fact way she'd said it. She'd scratched herself hard enough to leave scars, and she acted like it was nothing. "Why?"

There was a short pause, as if she was trying to figure out exactly what to say. "Because my uncle hurt me. More than once."

Marcos was having trouble keeping up. She'd said she'd made the marks herself, but that it had been her *uncle* who'd hurt her. That didn't make any sense. "You scratched yourself because your uncle hurt…" The dots rearranged themselves in his head, forming a picture he suddenly didn't want to see. But he had no choice. He'd asked Maggie to tell him—had demanded to know what those scars were. What kind of man would he be if he told her to stop now?

He braced himself to hear the worst. Every last terrible word of it. "What did he do, Maggie?"

She twisted her hands in her lap, not sure if she could go through with this after all. She'd thought telling him would be the perfect solution, but she'd never actually shared the whole story with anyone before, except for her therapist. She'd told her ex-boyfriend bits and pieces, but not the worst of it.

It was for the best. Once Marcos knew, it would be all over.

"My uncle abused me. Sexually. For almost two years."

"Meu Deus." Instead of recoiling, like she expected him to do, he gently slid his knuckles along her cheekbone. "How long ago was this?"

"It started just before I turned fifteen."

"You hurt yourself because of what he did?"

She swallowed, knowing she had to continue now that she'd started down this path. "No. I did it to force myself to stay quiet. To concentrate on something other than what he was doing to me. To prove that I could hurt myself more than he ever could."

"Shh...you have to be very, very quiet, Maggie. Don't make a single sound."

The memory of the terrible excitement in Uncle Tom's voice as he'd pressed her into her childhood bed crawled up her spine and lodged in her head, along with all the things that had come afterwards: the feel of her nails tearing at her skin as she'd fought to not make a sound; the control she'd felt when she'd inflicted more pain on herself than he had; the sense of release as endorphins had flooded her system, allowing her mind to override the humiliating things her uncle had forced her to do to him—the things he'd done to her.

The vicious cycle had been set into motion with

a single act. A cycle that had lasted for years after the abuse had stopped.

"He raped you?" Marcos's eyes were filled with outrage, but not disgust.

A niggling worry sprouted. This was not going the way she'd expected it to.

"Yes. He did."

"And your parents did nothing to stop him?"

"I never told them." She'd been going to. Then her uncle had died suddenly. And as she'd looked into her aunt's grieving face, she hadn't been able to bring herself to say anything. What good would it have done? Her uncle couldn't hurt her or anyone else ever again.

"Maggie...why? Why didn't you ask for help? Tell someone?" His fingers withdrew from her cheek, and she heard the faint tinge of anger in his voice.

"Because I was a kid. I felt powerless. My uncle was an adult and I was a child—I'd been taught to respect my elders." How could she really explain what had been going through her head back then? The sense of shame she'd felt for what her uncle had done—somehow feeling she'd brought it on herself. He'd accused her of that very thing, in fact, taking her hand and putting it on him, telling her to feel what *she* made him do.

Should she have known better than to give in to his subtle threats and demands? Probably. But she'd been grappling with her own feelings of sexuality toward a couple of boys in her class. And things had seemed so mixed up. So twisted out of context.

"I didn't say anything because my uncle died suddenly."

"I hope it was a horrible, painful death. In a dark prison."

His face was a tight mask of fury and Maggie realized it wasn't directed at her but at what her uncle had done.

Relief went through her system, the feeling in direct opposition to what she should be feeling at this moment. She'd told him the truth in order to push him away. Instead, he was drawing closer, and she welcomed it—tears springing to her eyes.

She touched his hand, starting when Marcos captured her fingers with his own.

Taking a deep breath, she continued. "He never went to prison. He had a heart attack. He was only fifty-nine at the time."

"*Only* fifty-nine." He pulled in a deep breath then released it. "He lived fifty-nine years too long. My God, Maggie, why didn't you say something that day in the car? Or at the beach?"

She shrugged. "I never told my parents. Or my aunt. Why would I tell *you*?"

The second she said it she knew she'd made a mistake. A quick flash of hurt went through his dark eyes, followed by his hand opening to release hers. She reached over with both of her own to capture it again. "I didn't mean that the way it sounded. It's just that I'd never told anyone about what happened, other than a therapist I talked to years later, when I couldn't stop hurting myself even after my uncle passed away. It threatened to destroy my dreams of becoming a doctor. Of helping those who can't help themselves."

Her fingers went up and trailed across the planes of his face, his fierce cheekbones, strong autocratic nose. Traced across his lips. "I should have told you, but I was afraid." It was the truth. And she'd told him today for the very same reason. Because she was afraid. Marcos's throat moved with a quick, jerky swallow. "You said you hurt yourself in order to stay quiet. Is that why you're so quiet now? Why you seem uncomfortable with noise, like at the subway?"

"Yes. My uncle didn't want anyone to hear us." He knew the worst of it. Why try to hide the other stuff? "I'm okay most of the time. It's just when I read something in the paper or come across a patient at the hospital who's been abused that it hits me—the realization that there are other kids out there just like me. Who are suffering the very thing I once suffered. And knowing there's nothing I can do to help them."

She paused to take a breath. "You've seen me curl my fingers into my legs. The temptation to self-injure is still there just beneath the surface. It's something I think I'll always struggle with. It's why I keep these so short." She held up one of her hands to display ugly, stubby nails—the acrylics from the ballet already long gone. "Good thing I'm a doctor, right? No one expects me to have long elegant fingernails."

Marcos tugged her hand toward him, his index fingers sliding along hers. "You have long elegant fingers instead." He kissed each of her fingertips.

There was something painfully sweet about seeing him do that after what she'd just shared. As was the fact that he wasn't gripping the steering-wheel, knuckles white, as he waited for the first available opportunity to tear out of that parking space. To slowly withdraw, like her ex-boyfriend had done. Or, worse, dump her off at home with a relieved goodbye, never to see her outside the hospital ever again.

Because she realized, despite all her reasons

for telling him about her past, she did want to see him, despite the risks. He made her feel safe. Wanted.

Normal.

Even if what they had was only temporary.

She'd never meet anyone like Marcos again. No one made her heart pound quite as hard, made her stomach wind up in anticipation of his touch.

"You're not running away," she murmured, half-afraid she was dreaming all of this.

"No. Why would I?"

She pulled her hand back down to her lap. "It's not every day you run across someone like me."

"No. It's not." He laid a finger across her lips, shushing her before she could assign a meaning to his words. "And it has nothing to do with your uncle or what happened to you. Do you think you're the only one who feels shame or regret about their past?"

"No, of course not."

"I have things I hide from people too. You asked about Sophia, once, about how we met..." Marcos glanced to the side as a police officer drove by their car then slowed down. "I think we should move before they decide to send for a tow truck."

"Do you want to go back to my apartment and talk?"

His lips quirked. "I was thinking along those same lines, but for an entirely different reason. But only if you want to."

"I do." Maggie smiled back, relief singing through her system, the delicious quivery feeling in her stomach returning with a vengeance at the look he gave her. "Maybe there's time for both. Talking...*and* the other."

He leaned over and gave her a soft kiss. "Maybe there is at that."

CHAPTER FIFTEEN

MARCOS PACED AS Maggie brewed coffee.

He'd made a quick call to Sophia, who'd assured him all she wanted to do was sleep. Her head still ached, but the pills he'd prescribed her were dulling it enough to let her rest. He promised to be back before bedtime.

Which meant time was at a premium. No overnight stays. Besides, he was having second thoughts about sharing the gory details of his own past. No, he'd never been abused. He'd been well loved, in fact. But to tell her he'd started out life as a garbage picker who'd lived in a squalid shack on the side of a hill?

He shuddered, remembering what she'd said about those handcarts needing to be outlawed. To tell her his father had thrown his weight against the front bar of one of those very carts, struggling to get it up one hill after another? About how their very survival had depended on every member of the family pitching in to help? How he'd ridden on one of those very carts many times?

If they were at his apartment, he could simply hand her the worn photograph on his television stand and let her see the evidence for herself. But they weren't, and Marcos wasn't sure if his courage was going to hold out. No one at the hospital besides Sophia knew his secret.

Maggie came out with a tray that held a thermal pitcher, a couple of mugs, sugar and milk. There was also a plate of cookies on the side. He took the tray from her, raising his brow in question.

"Just put it on the coffee table, please."

He carried it over to a low table made out of worn slats of wood. Some of the slats were painted pale blue and sanded to give them a rustic appearance, while other boards were stained a dark walnut. Others had been left in their natural state, alternating with the other two finishes. The table was then burnished to a warm sheen. He gave a half-smile. It was always interesting that the very things the poor used out of necessity could be found in high-end homes and bore equally high-end price tags. He vaguely remembered a dining room table his father had put together out of multi-colored slats of wood he'd dug out of the garbage.

Marcos was drawn to sleek modern furniture

for that exact reason. It looked nothing like what he'd grown up with. Rustic furniture of any kind made him feel uneasy—reminded him too much of his past.

"What?" Maggie's voice brought him back to reality, and made him realize he was hovering over the table without actually setting the tray down.

"Just wondering where you bought your table." He couldn't think of anything tactful to say.

"I bought it at one of those *moveis rústicos* booths at the hippie fair. Do you like it?"

Tension made his lips curl into something that resembled a smile but which felt a whole lot different on the inside. The hippie fair—so called because it was an artsy outdoor collection of vendors who sold everything from crafts to jewelry to furniture—just like the piece of furniture in Maggie's living room. The second part of her comment was much harder.

Did he like it?

He set the tray down, trying to think of an answer. He could appreciate the creativity that had gone into the making of the table, just as he could appreciate the ingenuity behind a lot of handcrafted items here: Christmas trees made out of the bottoms of two-liter soda bottles; paper swans fashioned from hundreds of painstakingly folded sections of magazines; purses made from the pull tabs of soda cans and crocheted together. But that didn't mean he wanted to have any of those items in his house.

Maybe it was like Maggie and her fear of going back to hurting herself. She kept her nails cut ultra-short to prevent any temptation. Well, he didn't keep around many reminders of his past.

"It looks similar to something my family used to have." There. He'd said it without giving an opinion one way or the other.

"I thought you grew up in an orph…" She dropped on the sofa, hands in her lap, while Marcos slowly deciphered her words.

When he did, he rolled his eyes. "Sophia?"

"I'm sorry, Marcos. She thought I already knew. It just kind of slipped out."

"Kind of like now."

"Please sit down. You're making me nervous." She waited until he sat next to her before continuing. "Don't be mad at her. I wasn't supposed to say anything unless you told me."

Sophia had never made that kind of slip before, so he had no doubt that what Maggie said was true. But he couldn't help the little spurt of acid that pooled in his stomach. What else did Maggie know? "What exactly did Sophia say?"

"Just that you grew up together in an orphanage. Did you go there as a baby?" She poured coffee into both of the mugs. "Milk and sugar?"

"Black is fine." He accepted the cup from her, fingertips brushing hers as she handed it over. She pulled back quickly, and he found himself frowning. "No, I was six when I wound up at the orphanage."

So she didn't know that he'd spent the first years of his life in a *favela*.

"You said your family had a table like this one? You have siblings?"

Why had he not thought about where this would lead when he'd agreed to come back here? For one thing, he'd thought they'd end up in bed pretty quickly. For another, he'd been full of bravado back at the park, but when it came down to sharing the nitty-gritty details of his own past, he was having a hard time making himself tell her.

"I have—or was it had?—a brother. He was adopted six months after we arrived at the home."

"And you weren't?"

"No. It's one of those things. It happens. He was cuter than I was, evidently." Somehow saying that made it sound trite, like they had all been puppies at a pound, every child vying for a chance to be taken home first. He knew that wasn't really how things worked. He was grateful for every adoptive family that gave a kid a chance at a normal life.

Maggie took a slow sip of coffee as if thinking about what to say. "It's sad to separate brothers, especially at such a young age."

"Maybe they thought it would be easier because we were younger."

"But it wasn't." She curled her fingers around her cup. "Do you still keep in touch with him?"

"I haven't seen him since the day he left." The little prick of pain was just as acute now as it had been back then.

"Oh, no! Surely the orphanage would know something about where he went."

"They tried looking into it once I turned eighteen, but the records were sealed. I don't even know the adoptive parents' names." The ache from those frustrating days never quite went away. "Graciela—the patient who called me Markinho— said she knew the couple was kind and that they would be good to him." But none of that made up for not knowing what had become of him.

Marcos took a big gulp of his coffee, welcoming the liquid heat as it burned its way down his esophagus.

"Was this the secret you were talking about? That you were raised in an orphanage? That's nothing to be ashamed of, you know." She set her half-empty cup back on the tray. "After all, look at you now."

The temptation to make light of her words came and then went. Because, really, it was dishonest. Especially after the bombshell she'd dropped about her own past.

"No. That's not the secret."

Maggie touched his forearm, the light pressure of her hand reassuring. "You don't have to tell me if you don't want to. I'll understand."

That was the problem. A part of him did want to, while another part desperately wanted to keep the truth compartmentalized in the tiny area of his brain reserved for this very thing.

Maybe it was time to set the record straight.

He set his cup down and then ran his fingers across Maggie's coffee table. "We really did have something like this. Only it was a dining-room table. And my father made it. Out of wood scraps he collected over a period of a couple of weeks."

Maggie nodded but didn't comment, maybe realizing that wasn't the point he wanted to make.

"We had one like this because we couldn't afford a real dining-room table."

"I don't understand."

He decided to just get it out there. "My dad

pushed one of those handcarts you see around the city. He picked up recycling items and delivered them to a man who bought them for pennies. My brother and I helped him sort the things he collected." He swallowed hard. "Then one day my father didn't come home. He'd been sick for a while before that. I think he had some form of Parkinson's from the tremors he had."

"You mean he died on the street?"

"I don't know. We were never told exactly how it happened. We just knew he died and that we had to live at the orphanage. They wouldn't even let us bring anything from our old house—although I snuck a picture out." He pulled in another breath. "We lived in a *favela* not so very far from the hospital."

"A *favela*?"

"The slum down the road." He forced the words out. "I'm sure you've seen it."

She nodded. "And your father… How awful. What about your mother?"

"She died when I was very young. The picture I have includes her, but I don't remember much about her."

"You went to the orphanage after your father died, then."

"Yes. A police officer came to the house…told

us to come with him. That was the last time I ever saw our home. My father never even had a funeral, as far as I know. I don't know if he has a grave."

"I can't imagine what that must have been like. How terrifying for a young child to be carted away not knowing where he's going." She'd withdrawn her hand a few moments earlier, but now reached over and threaded her fingers through his. "You said the slum was close to the hospital."

He nodded, not sure what she was getting at. "It's about a quarter of a mile down the hill. I do volunteer work there from time to time."

"Your father lived within walking distance of the hospital and never went in to be diagnosed?"

"No, he never did. That's what I meant when I said sometimes deserving people never get to see a doctor. He could have been treated had he gone somewhere. We do have public hospitals, but the waits can be interminable, and there's a certain social stigma involved with being a *favela* dweller."

She gave him a smile. "And yet look at you now, Marcos. You're a well-known neurosurgeon."

"Some people took an interest in me along the way, when I was a kid. Gave me a hand up." And he was paying that back the best he could every Tuesday morning, when he volunteered at the orphanage and did free healthcare clinics in the *favela*. "And I made a promise to my dad."

"A promise?"

"I told him I'd grow up and become a really good doctor." His heart gave a hard thump as he remembered Lucas whispering the very same thing.

Maggie kicked off her shoes and tucked her feet up under her on the couch. She then laid her head on his shoulder. "You kept that promise. Your dad would be very proud of you."

"Thank you." Too bad his success had come too late to be of any benefit to his father. He decided to bring this conversation back around to Maggie. "You've made a successful life for yourself as well, Dr. Pfeiffer."

"I still have a few scars, unfortunately."

He reached up to stroke her hair, liking the feel of her head on his shoulder, the easy way she curled against his side.

It felt like home.

Maybe a little too much so. But he wasn't about to dislodge her. Not yet. He wanted to soak up as much of this feeling as he could, knowing it would have to last him for a long time to come.

But the hours he'd spent with her gave him hope that maybe he'd be able to have a real relationship at some point in the future. Maybe even have kids. Maggie hadn't leapt away when he'd talked about his background. But, then, she wasn't Brazilian. Americans still held that romantic notion that anyone could succeed if only they worked hard enough.

Didn't you do that very thing? Succeed through hard work?

Yes, but he was the exception rather than the rule. Which was why he felt it was so important to help at the *favela*. Maybe he could someday help another child the way he'd been helped.

"Do you think you'll ever tell your parents about what happened?" He murmured the question in a soft voice, not wanting her to stiffen and pull away. Just in case, he slid his fingers into the hair at her nape and rubbed in slow, soothing circles.

"What purpose would it serve? They'd only torture themselves for not seeing the signs, for not stopping it. And my aunt…I don't think I could bear to see the look in her eyes, knowing that the person she'd trusted, that she should have felt safe leaving her niece with, hadn't really existed."

"Do you feel safe with me?"

She lifted her head to look at him. "I do. You're nothing like him."

"And yet there were those who thought he was kind and gentle."

"True." She blinked. "If you're trying to scare me, it's not working."

He eased her head back onto his shoulder. "No, *querida,* I'm not. That's the last thing I want to do right now. I want you to know you're safe with me. No matter what happens."

There was a short pause then her voice came back. "What if I don't want you to be safe? At least, not right now."

"What do you mean?" His pulse quickened just a touch as all kinds of thoughts went through him, most of them decidedly *un*safe.

"I didn't invite you back here just to talk, you know."

He smiled, even though he knew she couldn't see it. "No? And here I had these visions of trading secrets and painting our toenails. The skeletons in our closets could rattle their bones and dance a *quadril.*"

She gave a laugh that sounded free and maybe even a little happy. "A *quadril*? What's that?"

"It's like that dance that Americans do in a square. Couples prance around together. It's very popular with the Brazilian *gaúchos*—what you would call cowboys."

"Oh, a square dance." She wrapped her hands around his upper arm. "I didn't bring you here to do that either."

Yep, his heart rate was definitely off and running and funneling blood down to a certain part of his body. "So you don't want to dance. And you don't want to play it safe. I admit, I'm a bit stumped."

Maggie's head shifted and something warm brushed across the underside of his jaw.

Her lips?

It happened again. A butterfly-soft press of something against his skin.

Yes. Definitely her lips. And being alone in her apartment was sending his thoughts sliding down that little hallway to his right, where he suspected her bedroom lay. "You're treading on dangerous ground here, Maggie."

"Am I?" Her husky voice slid across his senses like the barest touch of silk. But it was as if she sent a message right to the heart of him. She wanted him. Despite her uncle's monstrous actions. Despite his life in the slums. This beautiful, brave woman was sending a quiet request. One he wasn't about to turn down.

"You are." He tilted her head back and looked

down at her for a long moment. "And if you're going to stop, you'd better do so now."

"What if I don't want to?"

"Then I'll have to do this." With his own muttered growl still vibrating in his chest, he lowered his head—did what he'd wanted to do to her since he'd found her sitting next to another man in that conference room.

He kissed her.

CHAPTER SIXTEEN

THE SECOND HIS lips touched hers she was lost.

No, that wasn't true. She'd been lost ever since that day in his car, when he'd taken her with a passion that had rocked her world. Far from being afraid, she'd gloried in the roughness of his touch, in the harsh press of his body against hers.

He shifted the angle of his lips as if knowing her thoughts weren't centered fully on him and calling them back.

And, oh…

His tongue nudged against her, asking permission.

She granted it without hesitation, opening her mouth.

Only he didn't thrust home, the way she'd expected. Instead, he pulled back just a bit. Kissed along her lower lip with slow, methodical touches of his mouth that made her shiver. "I want you to feel safe, Maggie. Always. Tell me you do."

He kissed the corner of her mouth, then trailed

across her cheek until he was at her ear. "I need to know you're here with *me*. At this very moment."

"I… I…" His teeth closed over her earlobe, robbing her of words and wrenching a low moan out of her that shocked her.

"Yes. That's it, *querida*."

His mouth moved back to hers, but again the pressure was light. Undemanding.

She wanted more. Didn't want him to be worried about hurting her.

More than anything, she wanted him to make her feel…not safe but fiercely alive. Like he had before he'd found out her secret.

Her fingers went to his hair and sifted through the dark strands. The bubble inside her popped, and the words swelled inside her. "I don't want to feel safe. At least, not in the way you mean. I don't want you to treat me with kid gloves."

He paused at her mouth. "What do you want?"

"I…" *You can do it, Maggie. Tell him.* "I want you to make me feel the way you did before. No holds barred."

He pulled back to stare down at her, a strange heat appearing in her eyes. "None?"

She shook her head.

"Oh, sweetheart, you may be very sorry you said that."

"I won't. I promise."

He pressed his cheek to hers, his right hand going to the back of her head and holding her in place as his breath feathered along the side of her face. "You make promises so very easily, Maggie. But this is one I intend to hold you to."

With that he moved, the suddenness of the act startling her, and she found herself flat on her back on the sofa, with Marcos leaning over her, his cheekbones tight with what looked like desire. Or lust.

Whatever it was, the change in his demeanor was like quicksilver, washing over her in a heated stream.

He'd been willing to do safe. To hold back. Just for her. But that's not what she wanted. Not what she needed. She wanted Marcos in all of his fierce glory. She had from the day she'd met him.

What did that mean?

She didn't have time to wonder, because the press of his body drove everything from her head except his presence. His mouth slanted over hers with a pressure that was just as sharp and sweet as it had been on previous occasions. His tongue finally slid home—no hesitation this time, only a hard, needy drive that set her heart pounding in her chest. She wrapped her lips around him and stroked herself against him.

He gave a muttered oath and shifted his weight, one knee sliding between hers, as he settled into place. Maggie's body had twisted sideways on the couch, her legs hanging over the side, but Marcos somehow fitted himself to her, mirroring her position. He was hard against the yielding flesh of her inner thigh. And what she wanted more than anything was for him to slide higher and close the six-inch gap and take her.

No holds barred.

Only her clothes were still on. And so were his.

She gave a soft whimper of disapproval mixed with need. As his tongue continued to invade her mouth, setting up a rhythm that made her quake inside, her hands went to his dress shirt, trying to wedge her fingers between their bodies so she could undo the buttons. Instead of helping her, his hands found her wrists and tugged them away, lifting them over her head and holding them there. Her fingers clenched and unclenched; she still felt no fear, only a sense of desperate frustration.

"I want to go slow, *querida*. We've done fast, in my car. We've done greedy, at the beach. I want to feel every inch as I sink into you, until there's nothing left between us."

His bald words made moist heat gather between her thighs, and she shifted, trying to ease the ache. There was nothing wrong with greedy, as far as she was concerned. Couldn't he see that?

Greedy was her middle name.

"I want to force sexy little sounds from you that you can't hold back. Sounds that are all mine."

All his? Something swirled around the periphery of her mind. Something important. Something that warned her that what she was doing was dangerous in more ways than one. But right now she wanted nothing more than to stamp out that irritating little voice.

She was made for this one moment in time. For what he was doing to her.

He leaned down and nudged aside the collar of her shirt, the breath huffing in through his nose as if he was trying to capture her scent. The sensation drove her wild and her hips lifted in response.

So caught up was she in trying to find some relief for the growing discomfort at the juncture of her thighs that she wasn't prepared for his teeth nipping hard at the joint between her shoulder and her neck.

"Mmm…" The sudden rush of sound exiting her throat was almost shrill with need.

His tongue licked over the bite with a steady

rhythm that matched what he'd done inside her mouth. And she suddenly wanted that tongue everywhere: back in her mouth; behind her ear; on her breasts.

"I love it when you sing to me, Maggie."

She had no idea what he meant and didn't want to bother working it out. But those little whimpers she could still hear were somehow coming from her. She wanted to make them stop, but she couldn't. It was as if Marcos was drawing them to the surface and teasing them out of her one by one.

"Please. I want you."

He'd talked about her being magic. That couldn't be right, because *he* was the one who was manipulating her like a puppet, forcing her to do his bidding.

No, not forcing. Coaxing. Cajoling. Enticing.

She wanted to grab his head and make him return to her mouth, but her hands were still imprisoned above her head. She tried to yank them free, but the effort was half-hearted. She'd wanted dangerous. He was giving her all that and more.

Suddenly, he levered himself off her, leaving her sprawled on the couch unable to move. She blinked up at him in confusion.

"You have no idea how much I want to take you right here. Right now."

"It's okay," she whispered. "I want it. All of it. Want you."

A muscle worked in his cheek as he stood there.

Without another word he hauled her off the sofa and into his arms, striding down the hallway with her.

Wait! He didn't know where her bedroom was.

As if he had an internal radar, though, he seemed to sense exactly where it was. Maybe her bed was giving off the same needy vibes as she was.

He set her down on the bed, head on her pillow, but didn't join her. She held out her arms in silent supplication.

"I wanted slow."

"It's okay, Marcos." Barely aware that she was talking, she only knew that he seemed to need some kind of reassurance that it really was okay. That she was fine with fast. Wanted it, in fact.

Maybe she could do more than simply tell him. Sitting up, her fingers—although shaking slightly—somehow found the buttons on her shirt and undid them one after the other, until it hung free on either side of her. Feeling wanton and, yes, *greedy*, the word he'd mentioned earlier, she took hold of either side of her shirt, shimmied it down her shoulders and pulled her arms free, until she was just in her bra and slacks.

How brave was she? Especially when Marcos's breath was growing more ragged by the minute, in a very audible display of need.

She was brave enough, evidently, because her fingers went to the clasp in the middle of her back and unclipped it. Not quite brave enough to fling the strapless bra from her body, however, because her hands went up and held it over her breasts.

Marcos gave a slow smile then unbuttoned his own shirt and let it fall to the floor. Unlike her, however, there was nothing that stopped her eyes from trailing over his firm chest, licking across his nipples, her tongue unconsciously swiping across her lips as various thoughts went through her mind.

Then his fingers went to the belt on his pants and all brain activity ceased, as with slow—and enviably steady—hands he threaded the tab back through the buckle, then pulled the whole length from the belt loops through which it exited with a soft hiss of sound. He laid it on the bed, then toed off his dress shoes and peeled down his socks, his eyes never leaving hers. Maybe she was supposed to finish undressing too, but she couldn't seem to move. Not even when he came over to kneel on the bed in front of her, still in his trousers.

"Finish me."

Her breath swept into her lungs as the double meaning took hold. Did he really mean her to use her hands? Her mouth? To make him lose control? Or was he asking her to finish undressing him? A fresh flood of moisture hit both her palms and the pulsing spot between her legs.

She started to reach for him, only to realize that in order to do anything, she'd have to let go of her bra, and it would fall, baring her to his eyes.

He'd seen her before, but this was in broad daylight.

"Do it."

The low intense tone made her muscles quiver and her nipples draw to hard peaks. He knew exactly what she was thinking. Instead of complying, she laid her forearm across her chest, and used it to hold up her bra, while slowly reaching for the button on his slacks with her other hand.

He reached down and gripped her wrist, drawing it up to his mouth and planting a warm kiss on her palm, before whispering against her skin, "You're going to need both hands for what I have in mind, Maggie."

Another hard shiver went over her. She'd never met a man as absolutely comfortable with his own sensuality as Marcos was. It was earthy and organic—and focused on her with an intensity she found unnerving.

Continuing to hold her hand, he crooked a finger for her to give him the other one.

She licked her lips, held her position for another couple of seconds then reached out for him, feeling the fabric of her bra whisper across her breasts as it fell onto the bed beside her knees. She ignored it, kept her attention on him as if by not looking down she could pretend that what had happened really hadn't.

Marcos met her hand halfway and gripped it with strong, confident fingers, carrying it up to his mouth and gently kissing it, just as he'd done with the other one. Then he joined her wrists together and gathered them in one hand, easing her back to the bed as he retrieved his belt.

What? She'd thought he said she'd need both hands to…

"Wait. Didn't you want me to—?"

"No. Not yet."

Her head landed on the pillow. "Then why did you need my hands?"

"So I could do this." He lowered his head and caught one of her aching nipples in his mouth, tongue brushing over the tip in haunting, gentle touches that made her back arch off the bed. She didn't notice until it was too late that the leather of his belt had wound around and around her hands until they were fastened together, the end safely looped through the buckle once again. Her heart rate took off as she realized he'd planned this all along. She was trapped. At his mercy. And she loved it.

Through it all, he continued teasing and tormenting her breasts.

She bit her lip as the sounds in her head careened wildly, seeking the nearest exit. They found it. Her breath came out on a stuttered moan that had his head coming up to look at her.

"*Deus.* I love to hear you, *querida.* That soft, sexy voice wraps around my gut like a vice. It makes me want to take you in a rush."

"Then do it." Maggie could not believe she'd just said that. Heat splashed into her face, but Marcos seemed not to notice.

"*Esta vez não.* I promised myself I wouldn't. And I always keep my word." The fingers of his left hand tightened as he lifted her bound hands over her head and pressed them into the pillow above her head. "It's why I don't want you free. You'll take me over the edge far too quickly."

The idea was heady. Did she really have that kind of power over a man like this?

Before she could let the sense of wonder wash over her fully, Marcos had lowered his head again, planting a single kiss on her other nipple. Then he shifted his attention to her slacks, and Maggie felt the button give way with a quick flick of his fingers. Down went the zipper.

"This is where things get tricky, Maggie." He insinuated himself between her legs, using his body to part them. "This is where you need to co-operate. Can you do that?"

She'd do just about anything at this point to have him inside her as quickly as possible. "Yes."

"I'm going to let go of your hands. But you need to keep them right where they are. Or it'll take me twice as long to finish undressing you."

She didn't want it to take twice as long, so she nodded her agreement.

Her fingers curled as he let go of her wrists, but she held very still, as if the slightest move could dislodge him from his task. Not that she could do much with her hands the way they were.

A quick tug at her waist had her pants and un-derwear over her hips and down to the tops of her thighs. He put a knee on either side of hers, pressing them back together so he could slide the clothing down to her calves. Standing, he removed them the rest of the way and let them drop to the floor.

"You are *lindissima*, stretched out like that." He gave her a smile. "Maybe I'll just stand here and enjoy the scenery for a while."

He wouldn't. Would he? As heady as it was to have a man like this call her beautiful, she wanted him on the bed. Now. "You wouldn't dare."

"Ah, but I would." His hands went to his trousers and undid the button. Slid down the zipper. Shoved everything down around his ankles and then kicked them away. When he stood, he was hard. Just as he'd been when pressed against her thigh moments earlier. "But I can do other things while I admire the lines of your body."

Still standing, he leaned over the bed and trailed his fingers along the underside of her arm, over the slope of her shoulder, down between her breasts. He made a complete turn around her belly button before slowly veering to the side and tracing the bone of her hip...her thigh until he'd made it all the way down to her foot. He'd hit nothing vital, and yet her body thrummed as if he'd stroked every erogenous zone she possessed.

When he made a leisurely return trip back the way he'd come, she could contain herself no longer. She reached down with both hands and gripped his wrist, bringing it up to her mouth the way he'd done with hers a few moments earlier. She kissed his palm, traced the lines with her tongue before deciding enough was enough. She wrapped her lips around his index finger and sucked lightly, her tongue stroking along the digit as she held him in place.

"Feiticeira."

Sorceress.

The muttered word was hot. Thick. And it messed with everything that was female inside her. Suddenly she felt wild and abandoned. Reckless. Because he'd shown that the tiniest attempts on her part could crack that iron will of his in half.

She released her hold and sat up, deciding to go for broke. But the second she leaned toward him, meaning to try the very same thing on his flesh, he backed away with a hissed breath.

"Not this time, *querida.*"

Like that. The hint that her touch was as dangerous to him as his was to her.

Raw emotion bloomed inside her, flooding every nook and cranny. A deep sense of…something. Something she couldn't quite put her finger on but that was beyond anything she'd ever experienced before.

Marcos came down on the bed, erasing all

thoughts of anything but his body against hers as he rolled onto his back, hauling her up and over him in the same movement—until she was seated on his hips, his rigid length pressed along all those sensitive areas that were squirming for attention.

"Do you have anything in this little table beside the bed? Otherwise we'll have to retrieve my wallet." He shifted, his hips lifting to slide himself along her, hitting the spot at the very top of her thighs and causing everything to clench down hard. Only there was nothing to clench onto. "And the last thing I want to do is leave this spot."

"The top drawer," she whispered, even as her face burned red hot at the fact that she'd gone out after their first encounter in his car and bought some supplies. She'd told herself she was being smart. Protecting herself.

He reached over and opened the drawer, his hand feeling around inside.

"What is this?" His eyes met hers as he held up something other than a package of condoms. Something she'd never meant him or anyone else to see.

"Oh, no!" She reached forward to grab at it, but her hands were still trapped together. Horror flooded her chest. How could she have forgotten?

That particular purchase had everything to do

with the man who was now studying the object with blatant interest. She started to knock it from his hands but he stopped her in mid-swing, holding her wrists in one hand as he'd done earlier.

"Maybe I should have tied your hands behind your back instead." Still holding her wrists, he ran the hard plastic tip of her so-called "personal" vibrator along the underside of her chin. Down her throat. Over one of her nipples. Her eyelids fluttered closed in reaction. "You continue to surprise me, Maggie. I never would have guessed. Where is the on button, I wonder?"

Her eyes popped back open. "No. Don't." The conviction behind that demand was feeble, even to her own ears.

"But I will. You told me no holds barred, remember?" He glanced at the bottom of the vibrator, and his thumb flicked something. The low, warning hum seemed to fill the room. "What do you do with this little treasure, *querida*? Do you use it here?" He skimmed the object over the tops of her breasts.

"Here?" He slid the side of it up the length of her neck and trailed it across her lower lip, continuing to talk to her in low, gravelly tones. "Do you know what I thought about as your lips were wrapped around my finger?"

She could guess, but there was no way in hell she was going to answer that question. Because to do so she'd have to open her mouth…and that suddenly seemed like a very dangerous proposition.

"Do you want me to use this on you?"

She shook her head, even as she felt his erection jerk against her as if he were thinking about doing that very thing.

"Oh, Maggie…I think you do."

"No." The word came out on a breath of desperation, but she realized her mistake too late when he was right there between her lips, turning off the vibrations even as her teeth clenched in reaction.

"Let me. Just a little."

What was wrong with her? Moist heat was flooding her insides, and she recognized she was as excited by what he was doing as she was embarrassed. Would he really use it on her? Watch her reaction?

He would. She knew it as surely as she knew she was going to open her mouth. And the anticipation wound up inside her until it reached unbearable proportions.

Her teeth parted an inch, then two.

"That's it, *querida*," he said as he slid the vibrator just past her lips and watched them close around it. "You have such a beautiful mouth. So soft. If you only knew how much I want it on me."

He slowly withdrew and dragged the moisture across one nipple and then the other, turning on the mechanism again.

She moaned as he continued to draw tiny circles around her breasts for another minute or two. Trailing the device down her stomach, the vibrations spread through her as he moved lower and lower, drawing it all out with torturous slowness. He let go of her wrists, but she had no desire to stop what he was doing at this point, even though she knew with a certainty where he was headed, and that the second he arrived she was going to come unglued.

Reaching the spot where their bodies were joined, he didn't put the vibrator directly on her; instead, he put it on himself—on those couple of inches that extended past her body. And she felt the vibrations all along her most intimate parts in a long glorious line. She couldn't stop herself from grinding down on him to increase the pressure, even as she noted the muscle working furiously in his jaw.

"*Faça,* Maggie. *Tem que voar. Por mim.*"

Do it, Maggie. You have to fly. For me.

The raw need she heard in his voice melded with

the vibrations and the motions from her own body, until they all rushed toward her in a single red-hot ball of fire. Her back arched, every muscle in her body heating as the flames carried her higher.

An explosion went off somewhere inside her, rolling up her spine until it came out of her throat in a long keening sound.

"Isso!"

Before she even had time to fully feel the effects of her orgasm, Marcos had tossed aside the vibrator, rolled the condom down his length and sheathed himself in her body with a shout that made her tighten up all over again.

Again and again, he guided her, hands at her waist as he drove into her, each time seating her deeper, the sensation of utter fullness completing the act in a way nothing else could and heightening the pleasure.

Grabbing her bound hands with his, he pulled her down onto him as far as she would go, holding her there as he groaned and strained upward with his hips several more times as he climaxed. He remained that way for a moment or two, before letting go of her hands to cup her face, his breathing rough, a sheen of perspiration across his upper lip.

He gently eased her down to lie across his chest,

undoing his belt and setting her free. Then his hands slid up and down her back in soft, slow strokes. "*Meu Deus*. What I've done…are you okay?"

The gruff concern in his voice made moisture gather in her eyes. Pressing her face to his shoulder, and letting his warm scent surround her, she did her best to blink it away while trying to gather the splintered fragments of her composure. In reality, there was no way she could appear untouched by what had happened. So she didn't even try.

"I'm okay." Her arms lifted to cradle his head as best she could from her position. "I'm more than okay."

It was true. She'd never experienced such deep satisfaction in her life. Or felt such a profound sense of despair. Because along with the physical release came the knowledge her heart would never be the same again.

Because she loved him.

CHAPTER SEVENTEEN

MAGGIE DID NOT want to face him today.

She walked across the parking lot of the hospital with slow, measured steps, adjusting her purse on her shoulder as she went. Every move was geared to take as much time as possible to reach the front doors. Her nerves were stretched to breaking point, since last night had gone from wonderful to terrifying with a single awful revelation.

The realization that she loved him had struck like a lightning bolt, seeming to come out of nowhere, along with the threat of waterworks. There'd been no way to stop the flood so she'd pulled away and run to the bathroom. She'd switched on the faucet as hard as it would go and let the silent tears flow for as long as she dared. But even a cold washcloth pressed to her eyes after she'd gotten control of herself had been unable to mask the puffy lids and pink nose. Winding a huge green towel that came down to her knees around her body, she'd exited the bathroom to find him already dressed.

He'd taken hold of her shoulders and gazed down at her for a long moment, while she looked anywhere but at him. Then he'd pulled her to him, wrapped his arms around her and squeezed. And then he'd left with a quiet goodbye.

Goodbye had never sounded so final.

She'd let him out, gone back to her bedroom and removed every trace of what they'd done together.

Well, every physical trace. Because the emotional one was still stamped across her heart. And she feared it would be for a long time to come.

A sense of melancholy had compelled her to pull on some running shorts and a light sweater, then she went out to her balcony where she leaned against the railing. Rubbing her arms and staring out at the lights of the neighboring buildings for what seemed like hours, she tried to figure out what to do about Marcos. Nothing came to her. The mosquitoes finally drove her back inside, reminding her she'd forgotten to put repellent on her bare legs. Her reward was several fresh bites that kept her company during the lonely night that followed.

Well you're here now. So it's time to face the music.

Maggie paused outside the doors to the hospital, closed her eyes and sent up a quick prayer for strength. Then she strode through the entrance, forcing a confidence she didn't feel in every clickety-clack of the high-heeled leather boots she'd put on to give her as much physical height as possible. Her feet would pay the price by the end of the day, but she didn't care. She needed to appear sophisticated, worldly, and able to brush off what had happened with a careless shrug of her shoulders. Just like she was sure Marcos did on a regular basis with whoever his latest conquest was.

She guessed that would be her.

The thought made her feel unbearably sad.

Making her way to the circular bank of elevators, she punched in the floor number on the central keypad and waited for it to spit out the number of her elevator, then she stood in front of the correct one, absently scratching at one of the mosquito bites on her leg. It was still early, so she was the only one in the area at the moment.

The elevator pinged within a few seconds and she boarded, resolute about one thing. No one would ever know that she'd stared down at her scars last night for a long, long time in front of the mirror and decided no man would ever make her do that to herself again.

That included Marcos.

She clasped her hands in front of her. He'd never

made her any promises, and she'd never asked for any. No matter how she felt, she was leaving in a matter of months. Then she'd be home, where everything was familiar, and where there were no sexy Brazilian neurosurgeons waiting to turn her world—and her heart—upside down.

The elevator doors opened and Maggie got out to see the neurology floor gearing up for a new wave of patients. She made her way to Marcos's office and knocked on the door, figuring he'd already be there. He always beat her to the hospital. Silence greeted her knock. Was he already doing rounds?

She went over to the nurses' station and found one of the early morning crew tapping on the computer and pulling up the day's scheduled exams. "Have you seen Dr. Pinheiro? He's not in his office."

She checked her screen. "I don't see any appointments for him, and he usually takes Tuesday mornings off."

That's right, he did. How could she have forgotten that? Maybe because she wasn't thinking straight these days.

"Oh, okay. Thanks. What have you got for me today?"

As the nurse went over the layout for the day

Maggie sagged, half in relief and half in disappointment.

All that worry and procrastinating for nothing. The man wasn't even here.

"Tia Graciela tells me your ear doesn't feel well." Marcos lifted six-year-old José Sousa onto the portable massage table he used for giving examinations at the *favela*. Brazilian children often used the terms "aunt" and "uncle" to refer to adults who were in authority, even their schoolteachers. He could remember calling Graciela "Tia" from the moment he'd arrived at the orphanage.

She was retired now. But despite her brush with the pituitary tumor, she still showed up week after week, whether it was at the orphanage or at the *favela*, to help him provide much-needed health care to those who were often shunned by society. It was one way he kept his promise to his father. José nodded, his bare feet swinging back and forth as Graciela moved over to the child's side and allowed him to grip her hand.

"Does it hurt all the time?" Marcos asked.

Another nod.

"How about when I do this?" He gently tugged the child's earlobe downwards, watching for a reaction. The child winced, right on cue, his palm coming up to cover the affected ear.

"Sorry. I know it's no fun to have someone poke and prod at you. But we're going to try to make you all better."

This time it was Marcos who gave an internal wince as he remembered saying that very thing to his dad, that he was going to "make him all better."

Well, he hadn't been able to help his father, but he could help as many of these kids as he could. The fact that he'd been born here gave him an "in" with the folks who still lived here. Not many people had the courage to venture down the dirt road that led to the heart of the slum, where drugs and police shootouts were common, and where HIV and STDs ran rampant. Electricity was siphoned to makeshift homes via clandestine lines strung in the dead of night. More than one person had been electrocuted trying to tap into overhead power lines with little or no experience. No one worried whether it was legal or illegal. Laws were for those who could afford to pay for what they wanted.

As hard as it was to come back here, Tuesdays provided Marcos with a way to remember his past, and he often heard stories about his parents from those who remembered them.

In a place where outsiders of any type were viewed with suspicion, he was lucky to be able to drive in without anyone saying a word. Despite his medical license and his expensive car he was still accepted by most who lived here. He was "one of the lucky ones" who'd made it out and who cared enough to come back for those who hadn't. Part of the responsibility he'd taken on included awarding anonymous scholarships to kids who worked hard. He hoped that would one day include little José, who he saw almost every week.

Marcos gave the boy's shoulder a light squeeze then unrolled his instruments. Slipping a protective sleeve over the tip of the otoscope, he showed it to him. "Do you remember what this is?"

"O—" José squinted, deep in thought. *"Otoscóp-scóp..."*

"Otoscópio. You almost had it. It's a funny word, isn't it?" Part of Marcos's goal was to teach these kids about his profession, including what tools he used and why. He could remember being fascinated the first time he'd seen a doctor's roll of instruments, only to have the man brush off his questions. He'd vowed never to do that.

For these kids, soccer was often seen as the only

ticket out of the *favela*—and they spent hours and hours honing their skills, hoping it would one day pay off. Marcos wanted to show them there was more than one path. Education was just as—no, *more*—important than soccer, since few kids actually made it to the pros.

The boy chanced a smile. "You will look in my ears with your *otoscópio*?"

"Yes. To see if there's an infection." He switched on the light. "I'll have to pull on your ear just a little bit, like I did before."

The technique helped straighten the ear canal and gave him a clearer view. He leaned down and peered inside. Red, inflamed tissue dotted by pustular material appeared, just as he'd expected. There was also a build-up of fluid inside the canal. He clicked the instrument off and released José's ear. "How about your other one? Does it hurt as well?"

"Only a little."

Marcos could feel the heat of a low-grade fever radiating off the boy's body. He glanced at Graciela. "How many of these infections has he had?"

She flipped through the papers on the table, finger skimming down the list of names. "Three so far this year."

"We might need to check in with a pediatrician about putting tubes in his ears."

Graciela winced. "You know how tight funds are for these families. It was the same way at the orphanage."

Jaw clenching, he nodded. He could remember how tight things had been when he'd been there. Beans and rice might be ubiquitous Brazilian fare, but when there was little else to go with them, even if the combination had been manna from Heaven, it still got a little old. "Let me talk to a specialist I know and see if we can get him in."

Marcos had pressed his colleagues for favors over the years. Most of them just gave a good-hearted eye-roll when they saw him coming, but he'd rarely had one turn him down. Most of them knew that they might one day need a favor from him in return.

And what about Maggie? Would he one day ask her for a favor?

What did she have to do with anything?

Hell, just when he thought he might get by without thinking about her for a couple of hours, there she was, her image hovering in the background just like the music he played in the operating room. Only, unlike that music, he found her anything but soothing.

In fact, he'd been careful not to bring her with him on these forays into the *favela*…into his past. Why?

Because she was only here for a couple more months, that's why. She wasn't a permanent fixture in his life—he'd never allowed her to be.

His teeth clenched even tighter. It seemed that anyone he lov—no, he didn't love Maggie. He changed the thought to something closer to reality. It seemed like anyone he *grew to care for*—there, that was better—anyone he grew to care for left. Whether it was through death or through adoption, there had been very little he was certain of in his life. He'd known from the beginning that Maggie wasn't here for good, so why had he slept with the woman? Held her in his arms and thought about what might have been?

Because it seemed like he was destined to make one stupid decision after another. Which might also explain why he'd had sex with her not once, not twice, but three damn times.

And that last time he'd upset her. Somehow. He'd seen it when she'd come out of the bathroom.

He'd pressed her too hard. Had gone beyond what she was willing to give. He'd even reminded her that she'd said "no holds barred" when she'd started to balk. And yet he hadn't stopped—hadn't paused to think about anyone but himself. Swallowing, he pulled his thoughts back to José, continuing his exam while trying to banish the pair of tragic blue eyes that had stared hopelessly back into his own. The ones that had followed him into his dreams and had dogged his steps all morning long.

Had she gouged herself after he'd left?

Deus. A muscle in his jaw spasmed, the pain welcome. That only made things worse, because it reminded him of Maggie's comments about what she used to do. About what he'd *seen* her do with those nails.

If he'd sent her reeling back to the past, he'd never forgive himself.

Well, that would be nothing new.

He'd never quite forgiven himself for his father's death either. Or for Lucas being taken from his side. He knew he couldn't have stopped either event from happening—knew it had probably only been a matter of time before his father had collapsed, even at home, setting in motion the same chain of events.

But just like Maggie scratching at those creamy white thighs because of things that had been out of her control, he still tore at himself emotionally for much the same thing.

And he had a feeling Maggie battled the very same demons.

At least she'd conquered hers.

Unless what he'd done last night had opened old wounds and tempted her to make fresh new ones. Physical ones.

How would he even know? Maybe he could talk to her, make sure she really was okay. Apologize, if necessary.

And if she refused to discuss it?

Then he'd have to find out the truth some other way. Because he needed to know how she was doing. If not for his own sake then for hers.

Because if she'd gone back to past habits, he might have to make one of the hardest decisions he would ever have to make.

He'd have to revoke Maggie's internship. And send her home to the United States.

CHAPTER EIGHTEEN

MAGGIE SAT PROPPED up against the headboard of Sophia's bed, thumbing through a magazine, while her friend ate lunch. She'd come to check on her after calling and hearing the other woman's pitiful voice. Thankfully Marcos was still at the *favela*, which was where Sophia had said he'd be. Her friend insisted she was fine, just bored. And she was planning on returning home within the next day or so.

Marcos's housekeeper was safely in the kitchen right now and well out of earshot as Sophia griped about the woman fussing over her ad nauseam. "I don't know how he can stand to have someone else in his house all the time. It would drive me insane."

Raising her brows, Maggie glanced over at her. "Are you talking about yourself or about Maria?"

"Hmph. I'm family. That's different."

Maggie grinned then settled into the pillow a little more. "So he volunteers every week."

"Without fail. He's even teaching any of the kids who are interested about different medical specialties. I'm surprised he hasn't asked you to come in and talk to them."

"Well, I'm an American, for one thing." She didn't say it, but for another thing she had no doubt that Marcos was avoiding her. Even when he'd come back to the hospital he'd managed not to come within fifty feet of her. She'd caught a couple of quick glimpses of him, but they'd exchanged no words.

So he was upset about what had happened between them. He'd get over it. They'd slept together before, and things had gone back to normal after a few days.

It hasn't been a few days yet.

She sighed and scrubbed at the side of her thigh with the tippy tops of her nails, grunting in frustration as it did little to stem the itching.

"What's wrong?" Sophia asked, glancing at her.

"I stood out on my balcony last night in shorts and forgot it's the height of mosquito season. I have bites all over my legs. And, uh…elsewhere." Those little suckers could evidently bite right through shorts, because she even had a couple of quarter-sized welts on her behind. Invariably, the spots would turn into grotesque bruised-looking areas. Not to mention the itching.

God, the *itching*. It drove her crazy. And she'd forgotten to take an antihistamine before leaving the house this morning.

She scratched again, for the first time wishing her nails were just a little bit longer.

Sophia giggled then grew serious and laid her magazine down over her lap. "Marcos warned you about dengue, right? You can get it even here in the city. You should put some repellent plug-ins in your apartment." She nodded toward the device in the electrical socket across the room.

"I have some—and I know about dengue. I thought maybe your headache had been caused by it." She drew her knees up and wrapped her arms around them to keep her fingers occupied. "How is it, by the way? Your head? I probably should leave so you can get some more sleep."

Besides, the last thing she wanted to do was have Marcos come home and find her invading his space—especially after he'd gone to so much trouble to avoid her.

"And leave me to Maria's nagging? Please stay for a while longer. Besides, my head is better today. And my neck isn't nearly as stiff."

"What time is Marcos due home?"

"I'm surprised he isn't already here." Sophia laid her head back against the pillows with a sigh. "At least Maria will have someone else to hover over once he gets home."

"Then I definitely should go."

"Why?" She frowned, then her eyes grew round. "Is there something going on between the two of you? I noticed he's been acting a little strangely."

Her brain kicked into high gear. She didn't want Sophia to start asking pointed questions. Ones that could quickly become embarrassing, especially if Marcos found out she'd spilled the beans without meaning to.

"Nothing's going on. We're just colleagues, which means I shouldn't pop in unannounced like this."

"You called me before you came."

Yes, to make sure Mr. High and Mighty himself wasn't home. "I didn't want to wake you up."

Just then the sound of a door opening and closing caught her attention. Her voice dropped to a whisper. "What was that? Maria?"

Please, oh, please, let it be Maria.

Sophia tilted her head to listen. "No, I think it was—"

Footsteps sounded on the tile floor of the entryway, along with the sound of low murmured voices. Then those same steps headed their way. The doorknob turned and the door opened.

She and Sophia glanced at each other.

"Hello, ladies. Having a party?" The lazy voice from the doorway made Maggie squeak in alarm.

She unwrapped her arms and straightened her legs. Damn. She knew she should have left.

The worst of the mosquito bites burned and she pressed her hand over the right side of her thigh, knowing the sensation was probably caused by nerves more than anything.

"Maggie felt sorry for me, so she came to visit."

Actually, Sophia had been the one to ultimately convince her to come, saying Marcos had given Maria strict orders to keep her there in the bedroom—by whatever means necessary.

"Did you, Maggie?" The low, husky voice called her eyes up to meet with his. After a tense couple of seconds his gaze finally moved, sweeping down over her body and coming to rest on something near her waist.

He didn't give her a chance to answer his question but pinned her with a look. "What are you doing?"

Oh! She'd known things would be awkward between them once they came face-to-face, but she hadn't expected the accusation in his voice over her visit. Did he think she was using Sophia to get to him? That she'd be so desperate to talk to him that she'd use any means necessary? The thought stung and for a second or two she couldn't think of a response at all, just sat there like a lump.

The itching became scratching.

"I don't know what you mean."

Sophia spoke up. "She has mosquito bites."

Huh? Why on earth would her friend bring that up?

Then she realized what he'd been looking at a second or two ago. She was clawing at her leg, without realizing it. She immediately stopped and forced her hand into her lap. "Yes. I've got a ton of bites. From my balcony last night."

Something flashed through his eyes. Suspicion, mixed with some deep emotion she couldn't decipher.

"Let me see them."

"What?" Both she and Sophia spoke at once, then her friend continued. "What on earth is wrong with you, Marcos?"

He shook his head. "Sorry. It's been a long day."

"I guess so."

Maggie was still too shocked by the demand to take part in the exchange. He wanted to look at her mosquito bites? Why? Not to mention the fact that she didn't want Sophia to know what had gone on between the two of them. She had a hard time believing that Marcos would be any less anxious than she was for others to not know the truth.

So he had to have been talking about something else. "They aren't from the mosquitoes that carry dengue. No white marks on their legs. Just the garden variety pests."

"Yes, those white marks serve as a warning." Again there was some strange intensity behind the words. Almost as if he'd meant them in an entirely different way.

"Can I see you outside for a minute?" he asked.

Sophia scooted up in bed. "What's going on, Marcos? You've been acting all *maluco* lately."

Maluco was a good way to put it. Maggie was feeling a little crazy herself right now.

"Nothing's going on. I'd just like to talk to Maggie about a patient."

"Aren't you even going to ask how I'm feeling?"

He quirked a brow at her. "I think that's pretty obvious. Besides, I called Maria a couple of times. She told me you'd been cranky."

"Cranky?"

She wondered for a second if Sophia was going to come off that bed and let him have it.

"I think she used a stronger word than that, actually." The thread of humor was still there in his voice. More than anything, Maggie wished he would use that tone when he talked to her. Instead, their conversations were like high-tension lines—full of dangerous electricity that could cut through body parts like a knife through butter if one wasn't careful.

"Well, you can tell Maria to kiss my—"

He held up a finger and cut her off. "I'd like to still have a housekeeper tomorrow, so if you could try not to insult her, I'd appreciate it." He nodded at Maggie. "If you can do without your friend for a minute or two, I'd also appreciate it."

She found herself rubbing at her bites again and having to stop before he saw her. He'd called Sophia cranky. Well, he was the *king* of crankiness.

Sliding off the bed, she leaned over and kissed her friend on the cheek. "I think I'm going to leave once I speak with him, okay? I'll check in on you again tomorrow."

Sophia glared at Marcos. "And maybe I'll be at my own home when you do."

He came over and gave Sophia a kiss on the head. "Let's discuss this once we've both had a few minutes to cool off."

So he was admitting he was a bit hot under the collar. Not that it helped her anxiety level at all.

He ushered her out with a sweeping gesture of his hand, and Maggie stalked through the doorway and headed for the living room, only to have him take hold of her upper arm and pull her down the hallway instead.

What the…?

Surely he didn't mean for them to have sex while Sophia and his housekeeper were in the house?

With the mood he was in, that hardly seemed likely. On either side.

He hauled her through the doorway of his bedroom and slammed the door shut.

"What are you doing?"

"Show me the bites." One hand went to the wall beside her, caging her in. His voice was low enough that no one could hear but them.

Still thinking this was some kind of excuse to get her out of her clothes, she drew herself as tall as she could. "I don't think this is the time or place for…whatever you're thinking about doing."

He frowned, his eyes raking over her face. "You think this is about sex?" His hand came off the wall, and he took a step back. "That's the furthest thing from my mind right now."

"Then why do you want to see my mosquito bites?"

"Because I don't think they're bites." He dragged

a hand through his hair. "Damn it, Maggie. I'd apologize for last night, but I wouldn't even know where to begin."

Apologize? Oh, Lord. He was sorry it had happened?

Well, hadn't she told herself the very same thing? Yes, but only because she'd realized she was in love with him. But that still didn't explain…

Her brain latched onto something.

"What do you mean, you don't believe they're bites?"

He didn't say anything, just propped his hands on his hips and stared at her.

If they weren't mosquito bites, what did he think they were?

Those white marks serve as a warning.

It hit her. He thought she was self-injuring again. Because of what they'd done?

"Marcos, they're mosquito bites. And there's no need to apologize for last night. We're both adults. We both wanted what happened."

"I…went beyond what I'd meant to do." The hesitation in his voice clawed at her heart. It explained his words from the previous night as well, when he'd asked her if she was okay. He thought he'd hurt her somehow. Emotionally?

She took a step forward to close the space he'd

opened up and lifted a hand to his face. "I wanted what happened as much as you did. You have nothing to apologize for. I promise."

"Then show me your legs."

He was absolutely serious—he wasn't going to accept her word that they were what she said they were. A deep slash of pain went through her, and she let her hand drop back to her side. Then she backed up. "All right."

If he made her do this, nothing would ever be the same between them.

But as she lifted the hem of her shirt, fingers going to the button on her pants and undoing it, she waited for him to stop her. To say he believed her. That he didn't need proof to back up what she'd said.

Of course, he didn't say a word, so she unzipped her slacks and hooked her thumbs into her waistband. "Don't do this. Please."

"I need to know."

Have it your way. She yanked her trousers down to mid-thigh, then stood up straight and proud.

"*Meu Deus.*" A litany of Portuguese words followed that low exclamation, the bulk of which she was sure were not meant for public consumption.

Puzzled, she glanced down at her thighs, and her eyes widened in horror. The three bites that had dotted her upper right leg were now angry, purple marks, crusted over with dried blood that had oozed repeatedly with each new batch of frenzied scratching during the day. Looking at her beige slacks, she saw the blood had actually seeped into the fabric. She'd had no idea she'd dug at herself that much. She'd have seen it, if not for the long tunic top she was wearing.

In fact, those scratches looked suspiciously like the ones she used to…

Her glance flew up to his. "Marcos, I swear to you, they're mosquito bites. I didn't do this."

Of course she had. She'd scratched them until they'd bled. But what she really meant was that she hadn't gouged her nails into herself to blot out other—deeper—pain. Had she?

No, they were bites. She knew they were. She'd noticed them last night as she'd scratched them in the shower. "I tend to have an allergic—"

"I've seen enough, Maggie, you can pull your clothes back up." His eyes closed for several long seconds as she did just that. When his voice came again, it was so low she almost couldn't hear it, and it sounded like it was filled with a wealth of pain. "I'm sorry, but you've given me no choice. I'm going to have to send you home."

"Home?"

"I won't mention this to anyone. We'll just say the internship was mutually terminated."

His words sank in and her stomach sank too, right through the floor where she stood.

"You're sending me back to the States?"

"Yes."

"But why?" Even as she asked the question she knew. It was because he didn't believe her. He thought she was like an alcoholic who'd fallen off the wagon. Hadn't her therapist told her it was possible? Why would Marcos believe her?

"Isn't it obvious?"

"They're mosquito bites."

The words shook, tinged with a desperation that was swarming in her chest and buzzing in her ears. She'd thought she'd have the next four months to prepare her heart for leaving Brazil. For leaving Marcos.

She'd been wrong. Her time was up. And the last thing she was…was ready.

CHAPTER NINETEEN

ONE WEEK.

No. One week, two days, fourteen hours and… He glanced at his watch… Twenty-two minutes since the last time he'd seen Maggie.

And yet the ache in his chest still hadn't subsided.

He'd handled things stupidly, but the sight of those ugly marks on her thigh had brought all his fears home to roost.

Mosquito bites.

They hadn't looked like the kind he got. But then again, he didn't scratch at them until they bled. But Maggie had sworn to him that's what they were.

He'd reacted without thinking, jumping to the worst possible conclusion and blaming himself. In fact, he'd had second thoughts during the night about what he'd said. But the next morning when he tried to call her apartment, the doorman had said she'd left unexpectedly.

"Left?"

"Yes, said she was called home due to a situation out of her control."

He'd repeated those words to Sophia later that day when she'd asked where Maggie was.

She'd given him an accusing look. "*You* did this. I don't know how or why, but you did."

Yes, he had. But he didn't know how else he could have handled the situation. If those marks were a result of her relapsing, then the best place she could be was at home where she could get some help—go to her own therapist. And if he'd somehow brought it on, then she needed to be as far away from him as she could get, because he didn't see how he'd be able to stay away from her if she remained in Brazil.

He took a half-turn in his chair and leaned his head against the back. She was like a feather drawn over his skin again and again—soft and gentle at first but becoming torturous if ignored for too long.

And he didn't want to ignore her. He wanted her in his arms. Night after night. He wanted to do things to her that...

That was the problem. She drove him crazy. Excited him like no other woman ever had.

He wanted...

Turning back around, he brought both palms down onto the top of his desk with a thud. He wanted her. For ever. That's what it boiled down to.

He loved her. Could finally admit to the emotions that had been festering inside him—maybe now he could lance them and drain the poison so the wound could heal.

Only it didn't feel like poison.

But if he was damaging her by being with her, he had to learn to live without her. Somehow. Although how the hell he was going to do that, he had no idea.

He'd done it before. He'd survived the loss of his father and his brother.

Hell, this wasn't doing anyone any good.

Just as he got ready to haul himself out of his chair, his phone rang. He swallowed, a tiny seed of hope struggling to burst free of its prison, just as it did every time someone called.

It was never her.

Pulling in a deep breath, he picked up the receiver. "Pinheiro here."

"Dr. Pinheiro, we've got a patient down here we think you should see."

He carefully crushed the seed beneath the sole of his shoe, before answering. "Head trauma?"

"No, shooting victim. Chest and leg."

"You need an emergency-room doctor."

"He's asking to see Dr. Pfeiffer. Says he met her at some medical conference you attended. I tried to tell him she no longer worked here, but he won't listen. He's kind of in and out of consciousness. We need to get him into surgery, but I promised I would try to reach you before we took him back." She paused. "Besides—and this is a bit strange—well, I know you're busy, but would you mind coming down here for a minute?"

The man had met her at the medical conference? Ah, hell. It had to be that Carvalho guy. The plastic surgeon who'd practically hit on Maggie. The last thing he wanted to do was see him. And how in God's name had he been shot? Probably wandering in places he shouldn't have been, like rich tourists who didn't realize what could happen.

The least he could do was go and see him. And he could have the satisfaction of telling him in person that Maggie was no longer here—and good luck in finding her.

"I'm on my way."

"Thank you, Doctor."

Just as the nurse had said, the patient was in one of the triage bays lying on a gurney, already hooked up to an IV and a unit of blood. Nurse…Anabela Coelho, according to her tag, was taking his vitals.

She glanced up. "Oh, good, Doctor. You're here."

The man in question turned his head, his eyes glazed over a bit, but it was definitely the man from the conference. The stranger's mouth moved, and he grunted out, "Great. Just what I need. The bastard doctor. I asked for Maggie."

Bastard doctor. Had Maggie called him that behind his back?

If so, she'd spoken the truth.

Marcos held his hand out for the chart, ignoring the stranger's words.

Giving a quick glance at the vitals, his lips twisted. Bullet wounds to shoulder and lower left quadrant of abdomen, moderate blood loss—two pints given so far. The patient had a compression bandage across his left shoulder, just above a tattoo of some type.

He moved over to the bed, taking a look at the name on the chart. He frowned and blinked a couple of times, his heart rate beginning to climb. "Are you sure of this name?" he asked the nurse.

"That's what was so strange. It's what was listed on his passport and his Brazilian ID. He says he knows Dr. Pfeiffer."

It couldn't be. It had to be a coincidence. All the same his mouth went dry, his heart still pounding in his chest.

Lucas Elias *Pinheiro* Carvalho. His brother's name…all except the Carvalho. He cleared his throat. "Dr. Carvalho? Do you remember me from the conference?"

The man lifted his hand partially off the bed and then dropped it. "Yes. You're the bastard. Where's Maggie?" the man continued. "What did you do to her?"

What *hadn't* he done?

He shook off the thought. "Is your last name Pinheiro or Carvalho?"

"Adopted name. Carvalho."

Adopted. His brain began swirling in crazy directions. Maybe Sophia was right. He really was *maluco*. Because nothing about this made sense.

His eyes went to the man's tattoo, and his breath seized in his chest. He recognized the rod of Asclepius with its serpent twining around a staff. Above the medical symbol were the English words "Promises Kept" and below it… *Deus Santo!* Below it was the name of his father: Carlos Rodriguez Mateus Pinheiro.

He felt the blood drain from his head and the world around him spun in and out of focus for a few seconds, so much so that he had to grab onto the side of the bed to steady himself. "Dr. Pinheiro, are you all right?" asked the nurse.

The man's voice cut through the fog. "Pinheiro. Your name. That was my name."

Marcos swallowed hard, a rush of tears flooding his eyes and blurring his vision. "My name is Marcos Almeira Pinheiro. And I think…" His throat clogged, and he had to try again. "I think you might be my brother."

A hand reached out and grabbed his wrist, and the man twisted his own arm—the tattooed one—gasping as the movement pulled on his wounded shoulder. "Is…?" He drew in an audible breath. "Is this your father?"

Marcos couldn't manage anything more than a quick nod, his insides all wadded up in a ball of spinning emotion and stunned disbelief.

The other man's fingers tightened. "Marcos? My God. It's true. I'm Lucas. Y-your brother." And with that the man promptly passed out cold.

Three hours later Lucas was still in surgery, and Marcos paced the waiting room, still in shock. He hadn't sorted through all his twisted emotions. He felt like his abdomen had been slashed open, his innards spilled out for all to see. The nurse at

Lucas's bedside had discreetly handed him a tissue as he'd stood there, staring at his brother's form as they'd prepared him for emergency surgery.

Only then had he realized his face had been wet with tears.

Sophia, recovered from her meningitis, had come down to join him as he'd waited. "I can't believe he's back, after all these years."

"He's not back. I'm sure he'll be heading back to America as soon as he can."

"But you're glad to have found him again, right?" Sophia grabbed his arm as he walked by and dragged him down to sit beside her. "Stop pacing. You're making me nervous. Don't forget I haven't even gotten to see him yet. Not that he'll remember me."

Marcos gave her a dim smile. "How could anyone forget you?"

"Well, how could you have let Maggie go without even a goodbye?" she countered.

Oh, hell, not that again.

He'd gotten nothing but grief from Sophia about what had happened with Maggie. Not that he'd told her anything except Maggie had decided to leave suddenly—no explanations. It was true. Technically. But his friend still believed he'd had something to do with the decision.

He had. And as much as he regretted jumping to conclusions without giving himself a couple of days to think it over—something totally unlike him—there wasn't a damned thing he could do about it now. Besides, he'd just about convinced himself it was all for the best.

At least, until his brother had appeared and he had started getting all kinds of weird ideas.

"Sophia, it'll do no good to keep rehashing this. Email her, if you want to know her reasons for leaving."

And he prayed Maggie would stick to the "mutually terminated" story he'd foolishly suggested. Because if she told Sophia the truth, his childhood friend would never speak to him again.

An hour later, Sophia had to go back on duty and Marcos was left by himself in the waiting room.

One of the surgeons appeared in the doorway. "Marcos? Dr. Carvalho is out of surgery, if you want to come on back."

He stood. "Is he okay?"

"Yes. We had to patch up an area of his liver, but we were able to retrieve both bullets with minimal damage. We've handed the slugs over to the police, but you know how things are in the *favelas*. No one ever sees anything."

He couldn't have heard correctly. "He was in a *favela*?"

The other doctor nodded. "The big one down the hill. He evidently got caught in some kind of shootout between the police and drug runners. Not the best place to stop for pictures."

That was *his favela*. The one he and Lucas had been born in.

Lucas had been there? Why? Could he have re-membered it after all this time? Their old house wasn't even standing any more, so Lucas wouldn't have found it even if he'd tried. But he had tried, evidently. His chest tightened. "Thanks. Which room is he in?"

"Three-oh-one B. Don't stay too long. He's still a little groggy, so he may not remember much about what happened." The doctor shrugged. "The police will want to interview him as well, once he's stronger."

Marcos went through the doors and made his way down the surgical corridor until he found the right room. Sucking down a deep breath, he went in and found Lucas awake, staring vacantly at the television.

He pulled up a chair. "Hello, Lucas. Would you feel more comfortable speaking in Portuguese or English?"

He had no idea if Lucas even remembered his native tongue. He'd spoken to him in English, when he'd first been admitted, just as he'd done with Maggie many times in the past.

But Lucas answered him in Portuguese, surprisingly alert, although his voice was gritty from the surgery and tinged with an American accent. "Either is fine."

Marcos sat by his bed, fifteen minutes turning to thirty as they talked about what Lucas remembered of their childhood—and about what had happened to him today. He didn't remember much. Just that he'd been in a taxi when he'd spotted a familiar area. The next thing he remembered, he'd been on the ground, his arm and side feeling as if they were on fire. That was it, until he'd woken up in the hospital.

Then came the question he'd dreaded. "I thought Maggie still had four months to go in Brazil. What happened?"

Marcos shrugged. "We both felt it wasn't working out."

"I'd just seen her not long ago. She never said anything about being unhappy."

For someone who was still supposed to be groggy from anesthesia, his brother was pretty quick on his feet. Then again, they'd been talking for a while.

His jaw tightening and molars aching even more, he gave another quick shrug. "Things change."

"I see."

"What do you mean?" Great. First Sophia. Now Lucas.

"I wondered if there was something between the two of you at the conference."

"There's not." He paused, knowing that just barely missed being a lie. "At least, not any more."

"I thought so. She seemed nervous about seeing you at the conference. In the way that a woman who's interested in a man might be."

"It was complicated." Guilt roared through his chest. Yes, it was complicated, but that didn't excuse what he'd done. Even his brother—a man he hadn't seen in almost thirty years—seemed to be able to see the truth for what it was.

As if to confirm his thoughts, Lucas gave a tired chuckle. "Complicated? No, Marcos. *We're* complicated. Did she break things off?"

"No. I sent her home. And she went."

"Why?"

The word echoed in his skull. It was a question to which there was no answer other than fear. Fear that he could somehow hurt her. Fear that she might disappear from his life just like his father and Lucas had done.

He gave an internal snort. Well, hadn't she? One day she'd been here and the next she'd been on a plane back to the States.

Because you put her there.

He'd been worried about her scratching at herself again, but when he got down to it, this had been mostly about him. About him not trusting her enough to accept what she'd said at face value. For not believing she would stay with him, if he asked her to.

Lucas's voice poked at him again. "Why, Marcos?"

"Because..." Hell, was he really going to do this with his brother lying there in a hospital bed? "Because I think I might be in love with her. And I knew she was going to leave, eventually. So I forced her out before she left on her own."

"You always were an overbearing ass. Even as a kid. *'Put these shoes on, Lucas, your feet might get cut... Do your homework before Papai gets home.'*"

Marcos couldn't hold back a laugh. "You remember that?"

"Yes." He closed his eyes with a sigh before looking at him again. "You can't control what happens in life, Marcos. You, more than anyone, should realize that. You just do the best you can, and keep your promises, no matter what. Looks like we both did that, at least."

"Looks like we did." They'd both kept their promises despite the odds against them. Two *favela* boys who'd made something of themselves.

Lucas grimaced. "I'd like to continue this conversation, but I'm beat. Getting shot evidently takes it out of a man. Besides, don't you have a phone call to make, an apology to offer…or, better yet, a plane to catch?"

"What?"

"This is probably the drugs talking, but if you love her, go. Make whatever you did right. After all, there's no guarantee you'll get two miracles in a row."

"Miracles?"

He nodded. "Us. Fate brought us back together at the perfect time. Don't count on it happening twice. This time you need to go out and hunt Fate down and make her do exactly what you want."

CHAPTER TWENTY

"Approaching the site of the malformation."

Maggie kept up an oral commentary of the surgery as she went. She'd transcribe the recording and put the notes into her patient's medical chart as soon as she was finished.

Keeping the catheter steady, she focused on the screen that showed the snarled network of veins that comprised the ateriovenous malformation located deep in Clara Gerard's cerebellum—a place where her scalpel couldn't reach safely. Creating an embolus in just the right spot was tricky, but by blocking the defective vessels they'd divert the flow of blood into the parts of the brain that were now being deprived. Hopefully that would alleviate the patient's seizures, which had been increasing in severity over the past several months.

She moved the catheter forward another couple of millimeters and studied the image again.

Maggie knew they might have to follow this procedure up with a blast of radiation to close the vessels permanently, but for now she was crossing her fingers that the blockage she was creating would do the trick.

Just like filling her days with work was creating a blockage in her own heart—one that prevented the pain from all that had happened in Brazil from reaching vital areas of her soul. But like her patient's embolus, it was a temporary solution to a very real problem. Right now, though, she couldn't think of a better way to deal with it. After two weeks she was still too raw to think straight.

"Preparing to inject the embolic material."

She could hear the faint rustle of clothing in the background as people moved from one place to another as they did their jobs but, unlike Marcos, she preferred to have a totally silent surgical suite. No music. Not much talking other than her own voice recording the procedure or asking for instruments. The vague thought went through her head that people must think her cold and unfeeling, although no one had ever said anything.

If they only knew just how cold she felt right now.

But unfeeling? If only she could be.

Holding her breath, she squeezed the plunger on the syringe, watching the screen as the glue-like liquid flowed into the offending vessel. The material was designed to harden quickly, so she should start seeing results right about…

Now.

The blood-flow pattern changed abruptly as the rogue vessels that had been siphoning off precious amounts of oxygen went dark. Careful murmurs went up around the room as others saw the same thing she did, but didn't want to disturb her.

Suddenly, she missed the open cheers that heralded success in Marcos's operating room. The slaps on the back, the loud congratulations. Marcos's proud smile as he saved a life that had hung in the balance—and when he'd aimed that smile at her…

She closed her eyes for a brief second as pain overwhelmed her.

Shaking it off, she concentrated on the job at hand. She still had to withdraw the catheter and finish her surgery. She owed it to her patient to give her the best she had. Several minutes later there was still no sign of blood leaking around the embolus. She withdrew the catheter and applied pressure to the entry site as she nodded to the anesthesiologist, who lightened the sedation.

Once her patient was awake enough to respond to questions, she gave the woman's shoulder a gentle squeeze and left to talk to the family.

The waiting room was crowded with Clara's relatives. Maggie smiled as she saw how loved the woman was. When they realized who Maggie was, everyone went quiet, and she gave a thumbs-up sign before she realized where she was. The A-okay gesture was perfectly fine to use here. But she couldn't bring herself to. Not yet. Maybe not ever.

She spoke with them for a few minutes longer, then gave a quick wave as she turned to go. She still needed to change out of her surgical scrubs and get cleaned up. She rounded a corner, her mind on what she needed to do that night, when she heard something behind her.

"Magía."

Her steps faltered as the quiet word wound around her with tantalizing familiarity.

She stood there for a second, uncertain what to do but unwilling to turn around and prove herself wrong. She had to have misheard. He wasn't here—had made it plain he didn't want her. And he certainly didn't think she was magic. Not any more.

She took another two steps before the voice came again, a little clearer this time. "Maggie."

A moment of indecision gripped her before she finally forced herself to make a half-turn.

Oh, God. It *was* him. Marcos stood in the corridor, hands shoved into the pockets of his beige chinos, a black Polo shirt hugging the hard lines of his chest. And those eyes. There was no mistaking those warm chocolaty eyes, the corners just barely crinkling as he watched her.

For a terrifying moment she thought he'd come here to talk to the hospital administration about what he *thought* he'd seen back at his apartment. Those mosquito bites he'd jumped to conclusions over. Could he get her fired? Surely he wouldn't be that vindictive.

Unless he thought he was helping her by ratting her out.

There was nothing *to* rat out, she reminded herself. Because she hadn't done what he thought she had.

"Why are you here?"

His hands came out of his pockets, and he took a couple of steps forward, stopping within three feet of her. Even though he hadn't invaded her private space, Maggie had to force herself not to back away.

"I came to apologize."

"Really? I thought you were here to ask me to drop my pants again." She stood straight and tall. "It's a little late for apologies."

"I know. But that doesn't mean I shouldn't offer one." He dragged a hand through his hair. "Can we go somewhere quiet for a few minutes and talk?"

Don't do it.

She knew her subconscious was probably wise, but she wanted to hear him out. Especially after the horrific two weeks she'd just had. It might be pathetic, but she wanted to be near him, even if just for a half-hour. There were so many things she didn't understand about what had gone wrong between them. Not to mention why he'd flown hundreds of miles to see her.

"Follow me." Conscious that her modest hospital was nothing like the huge one Marcos worked at, she led him back to one of the little-used exam rooms off the main corridor. Once inside, she shut the door with a quiet click. "Okay. I'm listening."

"I thought you might have started…hurting yourself again, because of something I did."

She frowned. "I'm not sure what you mean."

Leaning against the counter, while Maggie sat in one of the two chairs, he said, "I was feeling a tremendous amount of guilt after the last time we were together. I know there were things I did that made you…uncomfortable. But I pushed you to do them anyway. I worried that I could have brought back some bad memories."

"Bad memories?"

"You had one man who made you do things you didn't want. You don't need another one doing the same thing."

Maggie had had no idea that someone's jaw could actually drop, but hers did. "Are you talking about my uncle?"

"Yes. I was afraid you might think I was like—"

"No." She came up out of her chair and couldn't stop herself from going to him. "You're nothing like him. I can't believe that thought would ever cross your mind."

"It did." He closed his eyes for a second before opening them again. "And when I saw those marks, *Meu Deus*, Maggie, I thought I'd caused it all to come back. I was terrified. Stupid. I didn't want what I'd done to add to whatever scars you're carrying inside."

"You haven't. I loved every minute of the time we spent together." She offered a small tremulous smile. "I've grown enough over the years to say stop if I'm ever really uncomfortable with something."

He reached out and brushed a strand of hair from her cheek. "The vibrator…"

"I'm the one who bought it. After that first time we were together, in fact." She gave an embarrassed laugh. "I just never meant anyone else to find it. But I liked what you did with it, if you couldn't tell." Maggie needed him to know that she'd wanted everything he'd done to her.

"Then you don't hate me for what happened?"

"Hate you? Of course not. I was angry…no, furious that you wouldn't believe me when I told you what those marks were, but looking at it from your perspective—especially after what you've just told me—I can see how it might have appeared." Her brows went up. "I can assure you those bites are all gone now. Or do you want me to prove that, too?"

"No. No proof." He took a deep breath then blew it out. "I came to apologize, but I also came to ask you something."

She swallowed, not daring to hope for anything more than she'd had. "What is it?"

"Would you consider coming back to Brazil with me?"

Go back? Why? To finish her internship? Wasn't that just asking for more heartache? Nothing had changed. She still loved him.

She answered slowly, "I don't think that would be wise. I have…" God, could she really do this?

She had to. He had to know the truth. "I have feelings for you that would make any type of working relationship between us...awkward."

"What kind of feelings?"

Maggie could swear she saw something leap to life in his eyes. The little flicker of hope grew. "Romantic feelings."

Before she could think or react, Marcos had wrapped his arms around her and pulled her close. *"Graças a Deus,"* he breathed. He eased back to look into her face. "I have feelings too. Romantic feelings, as you put it. But it's more than that. I'm in love with you. I have been since that first month you came to work for me. I just couldn't see it at the time."

"You do? Are you sure?"

"Yes. It's why I sent you away. I couldn't bear to cause you any pain. I was also afraid you'd eventually leave me, one way or another."

The choking laugh that came out of her throat was a mixture of tears and joy. "I've known since that last night we spent together. It's why I bolted to the bathroom like I did."

"So much of this could have been avoided." The words were whispered, and Maggie wasn't sure if they were meant for her ears or not. Especially as his next ones were clearer. "I knew something was wrong afterwards. I thought I was the reason—what we'd done. I decided that was the end. I couldn't push you to sleep with me ever again."

"I was upset because I couldn't believe I'd let myself fall in love with you. I was devastated. And so very scared you didn't feel the same way."

He leaned down and kissed her softly. Maggie's arms went around his neck, and she held him tight, tears rising in her eyes again. She pulled back with a laugh and pointed at them. "These are out of happiness—just in case you get any other crazy ideas."

"I have many, many crazy ideas. And most of them involve you." He frowned. "But only if you'll come back with me."

"To finish out my internship?"

"Yes, that. But I'd like our partnership to continue long beyond that. We could use someone with your skills at the hospital. And I want to show you the place where I was born." His arms tightened around her. "I want you with me all the time. Will you come?"

"Yes." Maggie's heart filled to bursting. "I'll need a week or two to hand my patients over to another doctor."

"I'll wait. And when we get back, I have someone special I'd like you to meet." He opened the door and slung an arm around her as they trailed back down the hallway. "My brother."

Shock went through her. "Your brother—after all this time? You found him?"

Marcos shook his head. "He found me. Actually, he found *you*. And I can't tell you how grateful I am."

"I don't understand."

"Remember L. Carvalho?"

Maggie stopped and looked up at him, her eyes widening. "The plastic surgeon from the conference?"

"The same. His whole name is Lucas Elias Pinheiro Carvalho. His adopted name is Carvalho. He was shot and asked for you—"

"Shot?"

"It's a very long story, *querida*. One we'll have plenty of time to talk about."

"So you both became doctors. Just like you promised." She glanced up and tugged his head down for a quick kiss. "I think your father would be very proud of what his sons have accomplished."

Marcos didn't say anything for a long moment; in fact, he looked away, before scrubbing a hand down his face. But not before Maggie caught the glitter of moisture across one rugged cheek.

After a moment he started walking again, threading his fingers through hers. "I think he would, Maggie. I think he'd be proud of all of us."

* * * * *

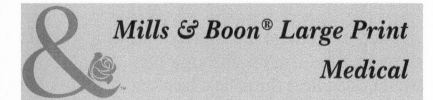

Mills & Boon® Large Print Medical

October

November

December

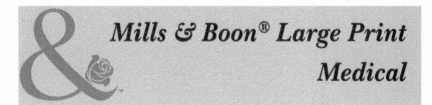

January

February

March